GIRLS IN WHITE

GIRLS IN WHITE

Rona Randall

CHIVERS
THORNDIKE

This Large Print edition is published by BBC Audiobooks Ltd, Bath, England and by Thorndike Press®, Waterville, Maine, USA.

Published in 2004 in the U.K. by arrangement with the author.

Published in 2004 in the U.S. by arrangement with Juliet Burton Literary Agency.

U.K. Hardcover ISBN 0–7540–6963–X (Chivers Large Print)
U.K. Softcover   ISBN 0–7540–6964–8 (Camden Large Print)
U.S. Softcover   ISBN 0–7862–6618–X (Nightingale)

The text of this Large Print edition is unabridged.
Other aspects of the book may vary from the original edition.

Set in 16 pt. New Times Roman.

Printed in Great Britain on acid-free paper.

British Library Cataloguing in Publication Data available

Library of Congress Control Number: 2004103445

CHAPTER ONE

In ten minutes Janet was due in Cunningham Ward and she would sample Sister Marlow's wrath if she were late. A stickler for time was Sister Marlow. A tyrant in so many ways. Nevertheless, Janet could feel no great concern, for she had just made up her mind to marry Augustus Bailey.

It was a pity about his name, but she could always use his second one—Phillip.

All things considered, she was really very lucky. She wasn't the kind of girl at whom many men glanced twice; her face would never launch a thousand ships, nor her figure challenge Betty Grable. She wasn't bad-looking—in a nice, ordinary sort of way—but none of the men who occupied beds in the famous hospital ever tried to date her after they left.

She was twenty-eight, staff nurse in Cunningham, and already the juniors were beginning to regard her as an old maid.

But these were not the only deciding factors in Janet's acceptance of Augustus Bailey. She was, to put it simply, the marrying kind—and Augustus was the first man to realize the fact. At twenty-eight a girl stopped dreaming of a knight-errant on a white charger. If he'd been coming, thought Janet, he'd have charged long ago.

She fastened the stud in her stiff white collar, forced another through the unyielding hole in her belt, donned her immaculate cuffs and prepared to go on duty. Reflected in the nine-by-four mirror she saw Linda Powell's untidy bed, clothes scattered willy-nilly, as usual. She'd get a black mark if she were found out. Hurriedly sweeping the whole lot into a bundle—fragile nylon, flimsy georgette, diaphanous chiffon—Janet hustled them into a drawer and slammed it. Lucky, lucky Linda to be able to afford such underwear—luckier still to be allowed to wear it when on duty! Elevated to the pathological laboratory as a qualified assistant, Linda Powell had stepped beyond the strict supervision to which ordinary nurses were subjected. She didn't have to live at the nurses' home if she didn't want to. She remained because she actually liked it—liked it, when half the nurses would have given their all to live out!

Nevertheless—and envy Linda as they might—there wasn't a nurse in the entire hospital who didn't like her. Especially Janet. They had been roommates for more than three years, which was a good test of friendship. Janet smiled a little as she hurriedly garnished the top of Linda's chest of drawers—powder puffs, lipsticks (how many did the girl possess?), innumerable toilet articles scattered there like snowflakes upon a mountain top. Linda had been brought up to be waited upon. It wasn't her fault that whenever she returned from leave she lapsed into untidiness again. In a day or two, she would realize that all those servants had been left at home . . .

Removing the last traces of powder from forbidden territory, Janet wondered if there was any truth in this rumor about Linda and Andrew McNeil. They moved in the same social circle, of course, and it was well known that the senior visiting surgeon was an intimate friend of Linda's parents, but did they really see him as a suitable husband for their vivacious, modern young daughter? What was even more to the point—did Linda herself?

Janet glanced at her watch. It was modest, but good—a twenty-first birthday present from her parents. It had been the best they could afford, and, because of this, Janet valued it even more.

Five minutes to go. I'll just make it, Janet thought, and sped downstairs. On the lower landing she met the ward maid doing home duty. She carried an armful of bed-linen and said with relish:

'New roommate for you, Nurse. Won't like that, will you? Betcha won't!'

Janet revealed her dismay.

'Thought you wouldn't be pleased!'

The ward maid spoke almost with relish. She bore the usual mild resentment of ward

3

maids toward the nurses, actually believing they did not work so hard as herself. She continued tartly:

'Your room was always meant to be a three-bedder, y'know. You've been lucky to have it as a two-er for so long.'

'You mean someone is joining us?'

'New nurse. Be a bittuva squash, won't it?'

It would, indeed. Let's hope she's nice, anyway, thought Janet, and dismissed the new nurse.

Hurrying across the courtyard which divided the nurses' home from the main hospital buildings she thought: *I'm engaged—or about to be! Why doesn't it feel different from this?*

She sighed a little, smiled a little. One can hardly expect the first fine, careless rapture at my age, she thought, and tried not to feel wistful about it. She concentrated instead upon Phillip's good points. His impeccable manners, his gentlemanly diction, his immaculate tailoring. He was the kind of man—forty-five and distinguished—with whom any girl would be proud to be seen. He took her to dine at quiet, select places. He ordered the correct wines. He tipped generously (somehow, the amount was never concealed) and nothing farther back than the third row orchestra was good enough for him. And as secretary-superintendent of the Royal Rockport Hospital, he occupied a respected position.

4

Janet Humphrey knew that many women would envy her. All the same, she could never call him Augustus. Phillip it must be. She murmured to herself: 'Mrs. Phillip Bailey . . . Janet Bailey . . .' It sounded rather nice. Very nice, she insisted as she hurried along the corridor to Cunningham Ward.

She pushed open the swinging door leading to the ward kitchen and saw, to her dismay, that Sister was there.

'You *are* late, Nurse!'

'I'm sorry, Sister.' What use would it be to point out that the extent of her deficiency was actually one minute and a half?

Sister Marlow clucked. She sounded like a fretful hen. She had tight lines of disapproval about her mouth and furrows between her level brows. Years ago her voice must have been young. Now it was dry and caustic. She snapped:

'What with you girls being late on duty and Doctor Rogers not sending down that test meal, I'm driven distracted! Nurse Blake, go up to the path. lab. at once and tell him I want it immediately!'

The door swung open again. A gay voice said:

'No sooner said than done, Sister! How's that for service?' And there was Linda, smiling gaily (as only Linda Powell dare smile at authority), extending the test meal, in its sealed container, upon a small enamel tray.

5

Sister took it. 'And about time!' she declared. 'What do you and Doctor Rogers do in that laboratory? Play Patience?' And she swung from the ward kitchen, her starched apron rustling with disapproval.

Linda winked at the student nurse, grinned at Janet, perched herself upon the kitchen table and said: 'What's new?'

Janet sent her junior out to the sluice. After all, the poor kid had to get used to it some time and there was nowhere else, at the moment, she could send her. Blake, the second year nurse, went hurrying down to dispensary with the dressing basket and the other student nurse was refilling carafes with drinking water. 'Dead Marines,' the sailors in town called them—their name for any empty bottle.

Janet took a deep breath. Now was a golden opportunity to tell Linda her news—but why was it so hard? She should be breathless, eager, ecstatically happy. Instead, she felt almost resigned. Not the way she had expected to feel when she became engaged. But she was past the age for dreams, she reminded herself. It was time to come down to earth. And the earth, once you came down to it, wasn't such a bad place to be.

Linda looked at her shrewdly.

'You're trying to tell me something. What is it?'

'I'm engaged—or about to be. He asked me last night. I decided this morning . . .'

6

Linda jumped off the table with a cry of delight.

'Engaged! Oh, Janet, how wonderful! And it couldn't happen to anyone nicer!' She seized her friend in a bear hug. 'You know how happy I am about this, don't you? As happy as if it were myself! Tell me his name! Do I know him? Oh, buck *up*, Jan!'

Laughing, Janet disengaged herself.

'Of course you know him. You see him nearly every day.'

'He's in the hospital, then?'

Enjoying herself now, Janet nodded. She did not know why she kept her friend guessing, except to prolong the moment. Suspense could be exciting, amusing . . .

'Yes, he is in the hospital.'

'Doctor Halliday?'

'He's married, goose!'

'Doctor Chambers?'

'Heavens, no!'

'I can't think . . .' Linda broke off with a little gasp. It couldn't be—oh, no, it *couldn't* be Brett Rogers? He and Janet hardly knew each other. Relieved, Linda dismissed the possibility of Brett and side-stepped her reason for relief. The pathologist occupied altogether too much of her mind—and her heart.

'Harry Horrocks!' she joked. Horrocks was the cheerful Cockney instrument man.

'Idiot!' laughed Janet. 'It is someone much

7

more important. The secretary-super., no less.'

'Oh, no!' Linda could not keep dismay from her voice.

Janet flushed. 'Why not? We've been friends for years. I thought you knew.'

'Friends, yes—but not—not—'

Janet turned away. She wanted, ridiculously, to cry. She realized in this moment just how much Linda's approval mattered to her. She wanted her good wishes, her enthusiasm—not this stunned silence. She felt her friend's hand upon her shoulder, heard her voice saying gently:

'Of course, if you are happy, I am happy, Janet—you know that. It's just a surprise, that's all. I'd always imagined you would marry someone different.'

'Different?' whispered Janet. 'In what way?'

'Well—younger,' Linda said, groping for words, trying to avoid the truth.

'He's not old.'

'No—not *old*.'

'Forty-five is young, in a man. And, after all, I am twenty-eight.'

'You don't seem it. Anyway, that's no age at all. Oh, Jan, you're not marrying him just because you're afraid—'

'Afraid of what? Of being an old maid? Why not say it, Linda? It's true, anyway. I am afraid of being alone when I am old—worse, of becoming like so many unmarried, elderly women in this hospital. Crabbed and sour and

8

cynical.'

'You could never be that!'

'Phillip and I have a lot to offer one another. Companionship and understanding and mutual respect . . .'

She broke off abruptly. Neither had heard the door swing open again. A man was standing there—a young, dark-haired man, clad in a white surgical coverall. He was tall and ridiculously broad—genuinely broad. Janet observed in a detached corner of her mind. Surgical coveralls never had built-in muscles.

He said: 'Sorry if I intrude—' but anyone could see he was not in the least sorry. He had actually been standing there, listening. An angry flush touched Janet's face and the sight did not perturb him in the least. He came toward them, saying: 'My name's O'Hara. Shaun O'Hara . . .'

Janet said frigidly:

'The new house physician? I expect you are looking for Sister?'

'I was. They told me I'd find her in the ward, but she isn't there, so I thought I'd try the ward kitchen.'

'And she isn't here,' Janet told him. 'She is with Doctor Chambers, I believe. She will be back shortly.'

'In that case, I'll wait,' announced Shaun O'Hara, 'but don't let me interrupt. Continue your conversation, please—it interested me.'

9

Linda stifled a laugh. The audacity of this Irish doctor amused her.

'I have work to do,' Janet stated briskly, and proceeded to do it.

Linda walked toward the door. Janet called after her: 'I forgot to tell you—we have another roommate joining us.'

'That's a blow,' said Linda. 'Let's hope she's nice.'

CHAPTER TWO

Entering the laboratory, Linda saw the fair head of Brett Rogers stooping above his work. He was studying a distillation which bubbled between a maze of transparent tubing, writhing like a colored snake from the condensing flask. She wanted to put out her hand and touch his bowed head, but dare not. He would be horrified if she did such a thing, for young Doctor Rogers had no idea how ridiculously his assistant loved him. Although they had worked together in close harmony for more than two years, they were still strangers to one another. Sometimes Linda thought she would never get to know the real Brett Rogers, the doctor who had fought and struggled to attain the position he now held, that of chief pathologist to the hospital.

His people, she knew, had been

comparatively poor—his father a struggling schoolmaster. Brett had qualified by hard work and scholarship. Sometimes Linda felt that he despised her because life had always been easy for her, presenting no obstacles, denying her any real necessity to work. Couldn't he realize, she thought wistfully, that luxury can, in itself, be as big an obstacle as any?

She stood for a moment watching him, and was startled when he said, without looking up: 'If you've nothing else to do, Miss Powell, you can work on that blood count for Doctor Halliday.'

She flushed, and moved toward her table. It was a long deal table flanking the whole of one wall, scrubbed and disinfected daily by the lab. boy. Brett's working quarters were at the other end of the room where he remained, for the most part, with his back to her. But he always seemed to know what she was doing, as at this moment. The laboratory door swung silently and her crêpe-soled hospital shoes made no noise, but he had known, nevertheless, that she had entered.

The lab. boy was right when he said that Doc. Rogers had eyes in the back of his head. A disconcerting place to keep them, thought Linda with an inner smile as she pulled out her tall stool and began to work.

Still intent upon the curling, colored liquid, he said over his shoulder:

11

'I'd like you to work late tonight, Miss Powell. I think I'm on to something which might help that case down in Drake Ward. I could do with an extra hand for an hour or two.'

Her heart leapt, as it always did at the chance to be with him after normal working hours, but—characteristically—he misunderstood her hesitation.

'An engagement, I presume?' He wished to heaven he could keep that note of sarcasm out of his voice when she disappointed him. He had counted on her help this evening. It meant a lot to him. So much that he was afraid of revealing it and, to cover up, resorted to his usual defense—sarcasm. It was easier to adopt a pose of critical disparagement than to let down the barriers of his reserve; easier to pretend indifference than to reveal the secret corners of his heart. Brett Rogers was more than shy—he was deeply sensitive; sensitive about his lack of social position in this town where social position counted for so much. Naval towns were like that, he had been warned before he came to Rockport, but it hadn't mattered—then. How was he to know that Linda Powell, daughter of the wealthy Powells of Heath Hill, was to come into his life and, for the first time, make him conscious of his humble background and lack of sophistication? There were moments when he wanted to hate her for it—but he never could.

He saw her chin shoot up proudly.

'I was going to say, Doctor, that I would be pleased to work late.'

'Don't put yourself out for me,' he answered briskly. 'I should hate to think that the social life of Rockport suffered any sort of eclipse on my account.'

She turned her back upon him, as she always did when he touched her on the raw, when his bitter tongue scathed her, when his mockery threatened to release the dam of her tears. Surely he must know how terribly he could hurt her, how his scorn and derision made her inwardly shrink, how his contempt for her comfortable, luxurious world made her feel ashamed. Wasn't that, after all, what he was really trying to do? He despises me, she thought. Very well—let him! But never shall he see that I know—or that I care!

She stooped above her work, saying indifferently, but politely: 'I have no engagement tonight, Doctor, so it will be quite convenient for me to remain for an hour or two.'

'I may keep you longer than that.'

'Very well. I will let the home sister know. The orderly locks up at ten-thirty, you know.'

'Oh, of course—you live at the nurses' home, don't you? I forgot. What is it like? Slumming?' When she made no answer he continued relentlessly: 'Quite a contrast to Heath Hill, at any rate . . .'

'Dorms are always a contrast to one's home,' she answered quietly.

He said, unexpectedly gentle: 'I'm sorry. I'm an ill-tempered brute. Forgive me, Linda . . .'

He was rewarded by her lovely smile—the smile which, had she but known it, had greater power than anything on earth to touch the isolated corners of his lonely heart.

He turned away abruptly, intent upon his work again, putting up the barriers of his reserve once more. Shutting her out. Rebuffing her.

Her smile died.

With averted face, he said abruptly: 'We'll eat first. There's a little place down by the waterfront—you won't know it. "Mike's Place," it's called. The food is good, and it is clean. Will you dine with me there, Linda?'

She was aware of a wild excitement, a tremulous joy. He might have been inviting her to the most exclusive club in London. She wanted to cry: 'I'd love to—love to, Brett!' But she took a deep breath and answered coolly: 'Sounds fun!'

He gave a short, bitter laugh.

'Yes, I expect it will be a bit of a novelty—for you.' And he turned away from her again.

*　　　*　　　*

When the door of the ward kitchen closed behind Linda, Janet said to Shaun O'Hara

14

briskly: 'I have work to do, Doctor, and I presume you have, too?'

He grinned disarmingly.

'Meaning that I am dismissed? But I am not so easily disposed of, Nurse. I am waiting for Sister—didn't I tell you? Unless, of course, you would like to take me round the ward yourself?'

She regarded him frigidly. She wanted to snub him, but could think of no effective rejoinder.

'I would hardly usurp Sister's place,' she told him, and began to assemble her case charts for inspection.

Shaun O'Hara straddled a chair.

'While I wait, Nurse, I'd like to hear more about this engagement of yours. Do I congratulate you? The sec.-super. is quite a catch, I suppose?'

Her cheeks flamed.

'You are impertinent, Doctor!'

'I know,' he agreed amiably. 'I always have been. You'll get used to it, in time. But the basis of my impertinence is friendly interest—please believe that. I was very interested just now, listening to the account of your romance—and your friend's reaction, by the way, could have been based upon sheer feminine jealousy. Women are like that, I understand.'

'Then you understand wrong! There isn't a scrap of jealousy in Linda Powell's make-up.'

'Different from me,' he murmured. 'I can be quite hellishly jealous, Nurse . . .'

She cast an indifferent glance upon him. She had met audacious doctors before, and knew how to put them in their place, or thought she did. But Shaun O'Hara merely grinned and said: 'Angry, Nurse? Not with me, I hope?'

Really, his smile was too disarming! No doubt he knew it and traded upon it. Resolutely, Janet turned away.

'I can assure you, Doctor O'Hara, that I am too indifferent about you to be angry.'

'A pity,' he sighed. 'Anger, like hatred, is an active, vigorous emotion—and you seem to me far too vital to be incapable of either. But still, there's time—'

'Time?' she echoed. 'For what?'

'Time to rouse you. To awaken you. I think I'd like to do that, Nurse.'

The man was a flirt, of course. He could keep his Irish blarney for nurses less wise than herself. She heard his deep, rich chuckle and knew a surprising desire to laugh with him. She had to steel herself against the infection of this man's laughter.

'All the same,' he said evenly, 'I don't congratulate you, you know. But I *do* congratulate the sec.-super. I haven't met him yet, but I look forward to doing so.'

Surprised, Janet said: 'But surely you reported to his office when you arrived?'

'He wasn't there.'

'But Augustus is never late!'

'Augustus? Oh, *not* Augustus, surely! Not for you, Nurse. I just can't visualize you married to an Augustus!'

She said coldly: 'His second name is Phillip. I call him that . . .'

She reverted to Phillip's absence from his office. That was unlike the conscientious man she knew him to be, but young Doctor O'Hara waved a negligent hand and said:

'Oh, don't worry about that, Nurse—a board meeting was in progress and I simply couldn't be bothered waiting. So I asked to be directed to my quarters and moved in.'

'You certainly don't waste much time,' said Janet, with grudging admiration.

'I don't believe in wasting time—unless, of course, I spend it in this fashion.' His eyes twinkled and he tilted his dark head upon one side, studying her. 'You interest me, Nurse. You intrigue me. I am frankly puzzled . . .'

Unwillingly, she questioned: 'About what?'

'About your reason for marrying a man you do not love.'

Startled, almost frightened, her head jerked up. He saw at once that he had hit upon the truth—not that it was difficult to discover, for her defensive attitude was revealing. And what was it she had been saying when he came in? That she was afraid of becoming an old maid, of being left on the shelf! He wanted to laugh aloud. Why did young women, often quite intelligent young women, regard the approaching thirties as terrifying milestones?

He said softly: 'You're so young—oh yes, you are, despite your years! So blessedly young and inexperienced. And so very, very foolish . . .'

The kitchen door swung open. Sister Marlow's harsh voice cut into the moment.

'Ah, there you are, Doctor! I heard you had arrived and were looking for me. I presume Nurse Humphrey has been showing you the case charts? Good . . . good . . . that will save me a lot of explanations as we do our rounds . . .'

And she turned, like a ship in full sail, and launched ahead of him into the ward. At the door, Shaun O'Hara turned and grinned at Janet Humphrey.

'Maybe you know best, Nurse,' he taunted, 'and I suppose a bird in the hand *is* worth two in the bush—even if it's only a sparrow!'

She wanted to hit him.

CHAPTER THREE

Once a week Matron made a tour of inspection. It was a nerve-racking day in the wards, for she demanded a standard of excellence bordering upon perfection.

Accompanied by Sister and followed by an apprehensive Staff Nurse, she made what was known among the nursing staff as The Grand Tour, and until it was over tension prevailed.

Shaun O'Hara left Janet feeling distinctly ruffled, which made things worse. On Matron's day she was particularly anxious to be calm and efficient, but the dark, disturbing eyes of the new doctor taunted her even when he had gone. She did not come into further contact with him until, during Matron's inspection, he appeared outside one of the private wards attached to Cunningham.

'I wanted to speak to you about this patient, Matron. I am not in agreement with his treatment. I disapprove of his isolation. I'd like to put him with other men, in the main ward.'

Janet heard Sister Marlow's smothered gasp. Newly arrived and in a junior position, Shaun O'Hara was asking for a snub. Nevertheless, in a remote corner of her mind Janet admired his courage.

So, perhaps, did Matron, for after her first glance of surprise a corner of her mouth quivered.

'And why, Doctor?'

'I think he is brooding—a bad state for any patient, and particularly in this case. Imminent blindness, especially in the young and healthy, is a terrifying thing. That boy is faced with the possibility of permanent blindness—and knows it. Is it going to help to allow him to lie there under observation, with no one to talk to but occasional nurses and visitors? With only the radio to relieve the tedium of lying in the dark? And he doesn't listen to that any more. He can't, he tells me.'

'He is not a neurotic patient, Doctor. On the contrary, young Richard Herrick is courageous and level-headed. I have known him many years. It was the wish of his parents that I should allocate him a private ward. Rest is essential in his case, especially at this particular stage. He may be operated upon later. I see you have been studying his papers, so you know what the trouble is?'

'A damaged retina—slightly torn and highly dangerous. The shields are essential at this stage, I know, to prevent the effort of focusing the eye, but do you really think it wise to isolate him in a private ward, Matron?' He gave his sudden, disarming smile. 'An ordinary seaman, too. I didn't know the ranks were so favored! Why isn't he in a naval base hospital?'

'He was brought here by special arrangement. Mr. McNeil, our senior visiting surgeon, is one of the few men in England qualified to perform the particular operation this boy requires.'

'And do you, personally, think it necessary to isolate him?'

Matron hesitated.

'I did not, I admit. I wanted to put Richard Herrick among his fellowmen. He is a gregarious boy and I feared the effect of solitude upon one so full of life. But I had to concede to the wishes of Doctor Heron, your predecessor, who thought his parents ought to be humored.'

'But why? They are not the patient!'

'The boy's father, Sir Christopher Herrick, is chairman of this hospital.'

Matron's voice was dry. She had never thought highly of Doctor Heron.

'But since Doctor Heron has now departed, I may take it upon myself to move the patient, Matron. Will you back me up?'

It was plain that Matron liked his frankness—equally plain that Sister Marlow did not.

Matron said briskly: 'I will back you up, Doctor! We will move him as soon as possible.'

Sister Marlow protested at once.

'But there is no vacant bed in the main ward, Matron!'

'Then make one. Move that youth in bed number ten—the last one at the far end—the moody fellow. I've observed he is not too popular with the other patients, and no wonder! He depresses them and I really don't see why patients should be depressed, nor why they should put up with one who is frankly ill-tempered. We will isolate him, instead, and let him enjoy his moods alone . . .' And her warm, humane smile peeped out. 'How will that suit you, Doctor?'

21

'Splendidly!' laughed Shaun O'Hara, and held the door open for Matron to pass through.

It was at this point that the secretary-superintendent appeared, walking with his brisk, precise step along the corridor. Augustus never strolled, never did anything lazily. Nor, on the other hand, did he ever rush. He seemed to have achieved the perfect balance between haste and indolence, and the consequent result was an air of purpose and dignity. Everyone admired Augustus, especially old ladies. They liked his perfectly modulated voice, his good manners, his neat appearance.

Because these were working hours, he spared Janet no glance. He was far too conscientious to allow his eyes to wander when on duty. He spoke courteously to Matron, then turned to Doctor O'Hara and greeted him, shaking his hand perfunctorily, letting his shrewd eyes, behind their pale-rimmed spectacles, take in the thick mop of dark hair, the happy-go-lucky expression, the mischievous tilt of the mouth. And he did not approve of what he saw—that was obvious. He considered the young Irish doctor quite definitely the wrong successor to the admirable Doctor Heron. He and Doctor Heron had always got along well together. He could not visualize such a happy relationship between himself and the newcomer.

Nor, if it came to that, could Janet.

'I trust you are comfortable in your quarters, Doctor?'

'I haven't tried them out yet,' said Shaun, 'but the one and only easy-chair looks comfortable enough—if I ever have time to sit in it. I'll let you have my verdict when I do.'

The secretary-superintendent frowned. He disapproved of levity among responsible members of the staff. It was as plain to him as it was to Janet that the irrepressible Doctor O'Hara needed putting in his place, and the best way to do that, at the moment, was to ignore him. Augustus inclined his head courteously to Matron and, turning upon his well-polished heel, walked away.

*   *   *

It was later in the afternoon that Matron sent for Janet. Apprehensive and curious, Janet hurried to her office. It was a severe room overlooking the main entrance to the hospital. Janet's feet were soundless upon the hygienic rubber floor and it was with something of a surprise that she heard Matron's voice echo almost loudly against the austere, silent background.

'Sit down, Nurse.'

Surprised, Janet did so. So informal a welcome hardly suggested trouble. Janet's curiosity now overcame her apprehension and she waited with greater composure while Matron completed some notes.

The moment came. Hilda Gamlin looked up and regarded the girl before her. She saw a clear-cut face, not pretty, but oddly attractive. An honest, frank, friendly face, framed in neatly cropped hair which curled about her crisp white cap. Nurse Humphrey was always immaculate, her uniform spotless; she was a credit to the hospital. Matron liked her and wondered fleetingly whether there was any truth in this rumor about her friendship with Mr. Bailey. He was a nice man, of course. Reliable and honest. A little dull, perhaps; a little pedantic; not really the sort of man she would have expected a girl like Janet Humphrey to be attracted by—but people so rarely married the partners one visualized for them.

She became aware that the girl's frank eyes were regarding her questioningly. Miss Gamlin smiled and said: 'Rest at ease, Nurse—you're not in trouble. I just wanted to speak to you about a new nurse who is coming to share your room over at the home. She is a student nurse and I want you to help her.'

'A student!'

'Yes. I know you are a staff nurse and that it is quite unorthodox to ask you to share your room with a tenderfoot, as it were, but it was at my request that she was put in with you. I consider that you and Linda Powell are the two girls who can help Meg Watling most.'

'I'll do whatever I can, of course, Matron,' said Janet, wondering why this particular probationer should need help more than any other. 'Is there any special reason?'

'One you will realize as soon as you meet. Until a few months ago Meg Watling was one of the prettiest girls in Rockport, engaged to be married, ideally happy. Then she was in a car smash-up with her fiancé. She was injured rather badly on one side of her face. When he saw her, after her recovery, her fiancé broke the engagement.'

'Oh, poor girl!'

'I've known Meg since childhood. She is sweet and utterly selfless. She let him go. Personally, I think she was well rid of him. Keith Saunders wasn't worth her little finger.'

'Keith Saunders? His name is familiar . . .'

'One of Rockport's social set—I've no doubt you've heard of him. He is well known in these parts. A play-boy, nothing else.'

'I'm sure I read of his engagement recently, in the *Mercury* . . .'

'To debutante Shirley Travers. It happened shortly after he let Meg down. He might have had the decency to wait awhile, but Keith Saunders never had any decency.' Matron, a native of Rockport, knew all the current gossip, and most of the people concerned in it. She knew, for instance, that Shirley Travers had set her heart upon young Richard Herrick,

25

son of Sir Christopher Herrick, chairman of the hospital in which his son now lay, awaiting blindness. Well, Shirley hadn't got Richard Herrick, so she had taken Keith Saunders instead.

Matron continued: 'Shirley Travers' people have money. Meg, on the other hand, comes from quite a modest home. Her father owns those nursery gardens upon Ferrer's Mount.'

"The Watling roses! They are famous in these parts.'

'And deserve to be. Meg used to help her father, but now she wants work which will bring her into contact with more people. She has courage. She came to see me herself and volunteered for nursing. It will be the finest thing for her. It will bring her into contact with greater suffering, greater disfigurement than her own.'

'She certainly has courage,' said Janet softly. How could one pity a girl like that? One felt admiration instead.

'Only half her face is scarred,' continued Matron. 'That makes it all the worse, somehow. The contrast is so great—like a rose withered on one side only.'

'But surely—plastic surgery—skin graft—couldn't these help?'

'Her father did what he could to help her, but despite the success of his rose gardens he is not a rich man and the national health scheme doesn't run to beauty treatments,' said

Matron sadly. 'Perhaps some day—who knows?' She rose, closing the interview, adding: 'I chose you and Linda Powell to be her roommates because I regard you as two sensible girls who won't make Meg conscious of her disfigurement or make her feel different from yourselves.'

'But Linda is so lovely! Won't Meg Watling feel that?'

'Perhaps. But she has to meet pretty girls as she goes through life—and nice, ordinary ones, too,' she finished with a smile.

'Like me?' Janet laughed. 'We'll welcome her, of course, Matron. Linda and I will help her all we can.'

Leaving Matron's office, Janet came face to face with Augustus. The corridor was deserted and, briefly, he touched her hand.

'I have been thinking of you, Janet. I want your answer.'

He had a pleasant, cultured voice. It was never raised in anger or indignation. When he laughed he did that quietly, too. One could never imagine Augustus giving way to his emotions, or losing his self-control.

He took off his spectacles and polished them, replacing them with a neat, precise gesture. Without them he was quite nice-looking. Better-looking, really, than that vigorous young Irishman . . .

'How long must I wait, Janet?'

She answered steadily: 'No longer, Phillip . . .'

'It is yes, of course.'

'Of course, Phillip.'

He gave a nod of satisfaction. What more could he do in a corridor which could be invaded at any moment? Suddenly, and recklessly for so reserved a man, he stooped and planted a brief, light kiss upon her brow.

'Thank you, my dear,' he said, and walked on down the corridor.

Janet stood still. He might have been thanking her for something quite unexciting, something he had expected, something he had decided to have long ago—in his own good time. Illogically, she wanted to cry.

A voice beside her said: 'So it is accomplished, Nurse?'

She turned, and saw Shaun O'Hara leaning negligently against a door. Was there no escaping this man?

'If you mean, have I accepted Mr. Bailey— yes, Doctor.'

'A pity,' said Shaun O'Hara lazily. 'That puts me to so much trouble.'

'Trouble?' echoed Janet, mystified.

'The trouble of breaking it off,' said Shaun O'Hara, and went on his way.

CHAPTER FOUR

Later, when Janet met the new nurse for the first time, she was glad Matron had prepared her.

Meg was sitting forlornly upon her bed when Janet entered. Her face was turned toward the window which looked out across the wide courtyard to the main hospital buildings. The Royal Rockport stood upon a hill, high above the town, and spreadeagled below was the maze of narrow streets which swept down to the waterfront like a pattern of lace. Beyond lay the harbor, dotted with funnel and mast, with giant hull and stern. Ships lay at anchor, like gigantic moths caught in the spider's web of the sea.

It was a lovely sight and one which never failed to thrill Meg. She loved this quaint old naval town where she had been born and had grown up. Keith rather despised it. He preferred London and had wanted to live there after they married. Of course she had agreed. She had always given in to Keith, because she loved him and because, in the end, it was the easiest thing to do. Was that, she wondered, why she had surrendered so easily when he came to see her that night—and turned away?

She didn't blame him. She understood how

he felt. Keith had always loved beauty—beauty in all things. In nature, in women; in people and places; in fast, streamlined cars and vast, white-winged planes and fine, luxurious yachts. Yachts such as the Travers family possessed . . .

A voice said: 'So you're the new student nurse? I'm Janet Humphrey—staff nurse in Cunningham.'

Meg sat very still—just for a moment. A tense, brief moment in which she braced herself. Now it could come, now she must face it—that first, hastily smothered reaction; the shock and pitying surprise. Or, even worse, the curious stare . . .

She turned. The exquisite, perfectly chiselled profile with its smoothly rounded cheek and clean line of jaw was duplicated by one tragically mutilated. Janet felt a swift and horrified pity, but she hid it well, extending her hand and saying: 'Glad you have come to join us. I hope you will like being one of the girls in white . . .'

Meg smiled in sudden relief and extended a ready hand. And her smile was so naturally lovely that it almost eclipsed the ugliness of her wound.

But surely something could be done? thought Janet. Plastic surgery, nowadays, was nothing short of miraculous. People had been given new faces when their injuries had been worse than this poor child's. She resolved to discuss the matter with Linda and wished she had been able to tell her about Meg in advance. But Linda was working late. She would have to meet Meg Watling quite unprepared. Would she meet her, as the other nurses did when Janet took the girl down to the common room, with glances of surprise and pity?

But Janet need not have worried. Not for nothing was Linda the daughter of Joseph Powell, former senior visiting surgeon at the Royal Rockport Hospital, now retired. Linda had met all sorts of people in her short lifetime: people who had sought her father's help privately, people in the public eye, people of every class and physical condition. When she met Meg Watling she bestowed upon her her direct, friendly smile, registering nothing beyond a sincere welcome. Good old Linda! thought Janet, relieved and grateful. She had always admired Linda's poise and assurance, but never so much as now. She could carry off any situation, meet any circumstance, without so much as batting an eyelid. The new nurse, reassured and happy, went to bed that night almost looking forward to the coming day, which was something she had not done for a long time.

Janet and Linda were alone together, briefly, when Meg took her turn in the bathroom.

'You know who she is, Linda?'

'Of course. We buy our bedding roses, at home, from her father.'

'And you know how it happened?'

'All of it. *And* the rest . . .'

'The rest?'

'Shirley Travers.'

'Didn't she step in and take the fastidious Keith?'

'Only because she couldn't get the man she wanted. I know Shirley.'

'And who was the man she wanted?'

'Richard Herrick, of course. He would have been a far better catch for our ambitious Shirley than the reckless Keith. The whole of Rockport knew her heart was set on becoming the future Lady Herrick. Some even said Dick enlisted in the ranks to get away from her!' Linda creamed her face energetically. 'Heigho!' she sang. 'What it is to live in a naval town! But there's often a grain of truth in the root of gossip—like mud at the bottom of a river. And don't the inhabitants of Rockport like to dig it up!'

'Linda, couldn't something be done for poor little Meg? Something to conceal her scars?'

'I don't see why not.'

'Matron said plastic surgery costs money— too much for the Watlings.'

'I see—'

Slowly, Linda began to wield a face tissue.

'Of course,' she reflected aloud, 'it does cost money. Quite a bit. All the same, I'll see what I

32

can find out . . .'

She wondered who would be more helpful—her father, or Andrew McNeil. She decided upon Andrew. He was more modern, more up to date than her father, who had retired before most of the 'new-fangled treatments,' as he called them, came into active use. Yes, Andrew was the man to consult. He was kind, humane, interested in every genuine case of suffering.

Janet said: 'Here she comes—' and at once they changed the topic. Janet climbed into bed and burrowed beneath her pillow for the bag of candy she always kept there. 'Coming over!' she cried, and tossed one to each girl.

Linda laughed.

'You're like a kid, Jan, stuffing candy in bed!'

She wondered how the sedate Augustus would react if his wife did the same. Dear old Janet would have to grow up when she married him.

Linda switched off the light, pattered across the bare linoleum to her own bed, mumbled good night and prepared to sleep. She did not want to talk. Not tonight. Not after her evening with Brett. She wanted to live again the wonder of that evening: the intimate, friendly little supper—an excellent supper, too—across the bare, scrubbed table down at Mike's Place, with Brett, for once, shedding a little of his reserve; the walk back to the

33

hospital through the dark, cobbled streets of the town (Brett had, of necessity, been forced to take her arm and she could still feel the strong, warm pressure of his fingers beneath her elbow); the quiet laboratory at the top of the high building in which they had worked together, undisturbed. They had been closer during those hours than they had ever been before; so close that it was hard to believe any animosity could ever exist between them.

Why did it exist? she wondered drowsily. And where? Only in Brett's mind; not in hers. And what caused it? From what strange, unaccountable source did it spring? That was something Linda had never been able to find out. It was as if, in Brett's heart, he nursed some secret resentment—either against life, or against herself.

She thought: I've got to break it down! Some day, somehow, I *will* break it down!

CHAPTER FIVE

At six a.m. a bell clanged through the nurses' home and ninety pairs of feet pattered to the long bathrooms; ninety pairs of hands splashed ninety sleepy faces; ninety young bodies scrambled into starched blue cotton and starched white linen. Yesterday's aprons were good enough to start the day with; good enough for bed-making and dusting and the sundry jobs which had to be attended to before Sister came on duty at half past eight. By that time the wards had to be spick and span.

At half past six the breakfast bell clanged and ninety pairs of thick, black, flat-heeled shoes raced down to the long dining-room, lining up for mugs of tea and slabs of thick toast and kippers.

Home Sister, always a little short-tempered first thing in the morning, rapped out the day's notices as if she were barking commands on parade, directing the new student nurses to their allotted wards, giving details of staff changes. Meg, a little bewildered by the morning rush, was relieved to hear she was in Cunningham. That was Janet Humphrey's ward and she had already learned, over at the training school, that the staff nurse could make all the difference in a student's life.

All the same, Janet off duty and Janet on seemed two different people. In the ward she was brisk, efficient, firm, rushing the junior nurses off their feet, hurrying them over their bed-making, taking a hand herself with the endless task—which was more than many a staff nurse would do. But she was exacting. 'Don't forget the corners,' she warned, 'and the castors, too. And for heaven's sake don't let Sister see that pillow-case open end to the door! Careful how you lift that man, Nurse Peters! And don't let Bed Number Five have

35

an egg for his breakfast, no matter *how* he begs! He has a special tray from the diet kitchen. Number Nine is an appendix, so don't go filling him up with sausages or we'll have Mr. McNeil coming down on us later!'

She smiled her friendly, encouraging smile at Number Nine, an apprehensive young man, and said: 'Eleven o'clock your operation is due, Johnnie, so I think you can have a cup of tea right now—but nothing more, mind!'

It was plain that the patients liked her. They bandied slang at her and got back as good as they gave. 'When you've dusted those bedrails, I need you,' she said to Meg.

Meg hastened after her into the private ward which adjoined the main room. She was a little breathless after the morning rush, and although she had been inwardly apprehensive about this first contact with the patients she realized that there had been no time to look at them individually. Entering the private ward, however, she was confronted with the quiet figure of Richard Herrick, and something about the resigned way in which he lay there, the world shut out from his bandaged eyes, struck at her heart.

'You can wash this patient, Nurse,' Janet told her, and Meg experienced a rush of gratitude toward a staff nurse who was considerate enough to let a nervous student wash her first patient in a private ward, instead of before rows of critical *eyes.* Grateful, too, because she stood by to watch the operation, not flustering her with criticism or advice, quietly extending a hand to correct a fault when necessary, but beyond that, not interfering. Halfway through she said: 'You'll be all right . . .' and to the patient she added: 'I can leave you in Nurse Watling's hands. I have jobs to do before Sister comes on duty.'

As she turned away the new house physician entered—an unorthodox hour to arrive, said Janet's eloquent frown. He was in the ward long before his time. He smiled at her with unruffled good humor and said: 'You are moving this patient this morning, aren't you, Nurse? I just wanted to check up.' And Janet answered tartly: 'I never forget instructions, Doctor!'

Shaun O'Hara laughed and went on his way, while Janet, with frigid back, went on hers.

Meg couldn't see the patient's eyes, but somehow she felt that they lit up with joy and relief. He spoke for the first time.

'Is that true, Nurse?'

'Quite true.'

Richard Herrick let out a slow, grateful sigh.

'You're tired of being alone,' said Meg gently.

'Sick to death of my own company—and my own thoughts.'

'I can understand that.'

'You can? But how? Have you ever been ill—for a long time, I mean?'

'Quite a long time.'

'You poor kid—at your age, too!'

'How do you know my age?'

'From your voice. It is amazing how, when you can't see, you interpret voices. They're very revealing. They tell you a lot about a person.'

Sensing that it was a relief to talk, Meg encouraged him.

'And what does mine tell you?'

'That you are gentle—and graceful.'

'Graceful!'

'Very graceful. Not only in your movements—I can hear them, you know—but in your touch. That is gentle, too. You have used your hands a lot, and delicately.'

'But not as a nurse. This is my first day.'

'Lucky for me,' he smiled. 'How did you use your hands before you came here?'

'I helped my father. He is a rose-grower.'

'A nice life. Why did you give it up?'

'I wanted a change,' she evaded. 'Your other arm, please—'

She took the strong young hand in her own and chattered on: 'Those roses on your window-sill—I expect you catch their perfume every now and then—are *Gloire De Dijon*, a lovely yellow, almost old gold. And these by your bed are *Prince Camille De Rohan*. They are deep red—warm and soft. Feel them—' And she guided the sensitive fingers to the petals, watching as they hovered, and touched,

38

and withdrew. She held the blooms close to his face, so that he could catch their fragrance. 'What does that remind you of?' she questioned, for somehow she felt it important that this sightless young man should discover things for himself, that he should learn to explore them from the dark region of his mind.

'Dawn,' he said unexpectedly. 'Fresh and dewy and soft . . .'

'That is what I always think!' she cried, and he turned his bandaged face toward her again and smiled.

'Tell me your name, Nurse.'

'Watling.'

'Your Christian name, I mean.'

'Meg.'

'Just Meg?'

'Just Meg.'

'I like it. It is young—like yourself. And sweet. Tell me about yourself,' he begged as she removed the bowl and towels and began to slip a clean jacket over his shoulders.

'Nothing to tell!' she said lightly. 'I am twenty, and have lived in Rockport all my life. Nothing important has ever happened to me. I am quite ordinary.'

'When were you ill?'

'Last year.'

'What was the matter?'

She buttoned his jacket briskly. 'Nothing much,' she told him, and added: 'I'll bring your breakfast now.' But when she turned away he caught her hand.

'Nurse—'

'What is it?' she asked gently.

'I'd like to know what you look like.'

He heard her swift, frightened little breath; so faint a breath that anyone else might not have heard it. But weeks of darkness had heightened Richard Herrick's sensitivity and attuned his ear for the slightest sound. And this one puzzled him. Why should she be afraid?

'I've told you—I'm just ordinary,' she whispered, straining to release her hand.

'Stoop down,' he commanded, and when she resisted he pulled her gently toward him, passing his free hand slowly over her face.

She held her breath. The strong fingers touched her smooth, rounded cheek, moved slowly toward her firm young chin, hovered a moment as, exploringly, he gently outlined her mouth—and then moved on. Moved on to the pitifully scarred cheek and brow, hesitated for one brief, imperceptible moment, and then withdrew.

He said softly: 'You're pretty . . . very pretty . . . Why did you call yourself ordinary?' His voice faltered a little. 'You're lovely, Meg.'

She turned away blindly.

'Don't go!'

'I must get your breakfast!'

'Why are you crying?' he asked gently.

'I'm not! I'm not!'

'With your loveliness you have everything in the world to live for,' said Richard Herrick.

He heard the door open. He knew she was going. He called quickly, gayly: 'And by the way, you have a delicious little nose!'

Stifling a sob, Meg hurried from the room. Her heart was beating with a new, wild happiness. She thought: Oh, I'm so glad, so glad he could not see me!

Here, at any rate, was one person who would not regard her with pity, or aversion. That tentative, exploring hand could not have revealed her secret to him; in his sightless eyes she was beautiful.

*   *   *

It was late morning when Linda was sitting on her high stool, mounting fragments of tissue which Brett, with his incomparable and delicate touch, had frozen and cut. They were like alabaster, she thought, marvelling, as always, at their color and formation. It was Brett who had revealed this beauty to her. She no longer quelled a secret shudder when she handled a section. 'They're exquisite, aren't they?' he had once said. 'It takes nature to create such perfection of color, such delicate formation . . .' After that, she had seen through his eyes and thought with his mind. Through her microscope she saw the knots of bacteria as jewels of color, as he had once

41

described them. In Brett's scientific mind there was a poetic streak, a love and appreciation of beauty. Perhaps it was this which endeared him to her, which made her seek beneath his surface veneer of cynicism.

Andrew McNeil paused beside her, glancing over her shoulder and saying: 'That looks interesting—beautifully cut—'

She answered: 'Doctor Rogers did it—I am merely mounting. I haven't advanced to cutting and freezing yet . . .' She was quite unaware, when she spoke of Doctor Rogers, of the pride her voice revealed, but Andrew McNeil, middle-aged and shrewd, noticed it. He noticed a great deal more than people imagined. He knew everyone in the hospital— or of them—and observed their progress. It was he who had first recognized Brett Roger's brilliance and had marked him for promotion. As senior visiting surgeon he had great influence, and if a person was recommended by him, they were made.

He had his eye on O'Hara now, and it was he who had encouraged in Linda her desire for a career, he who upheld her in the face of parental opposition, he who had realized that the daughter of the elegant Elizabeth Powell resembled her mother only in looks and had inherited her father's interest in medicine. Mrs. Powell's ambitions for her daughter were obvious—a successful marriage and an early one—but Linda, it seemed, had other ideas.

It had amused Andrew, in a way, to forestall the calculating Elizabeth. He well knew of her schemes, well knew that she hoped for a marriage between himself and Linda. He wondered if Linda had guessed also, and if she found the idea as ridiculous as he did.

If he ever married, which seemed doubtful, it would not be a woman nearly twenty years younger than himself. And if Linda ever married, which seemed obvious, it would be someone of her own choice and generation. She would not choose social position, either. He admired her for that. What type of man would she choose? One like Doctor Rogers? Why not? She was proud of working for him, and out of such a feeling anything might grow.

Andrew smiled at her—a kindly, intimate smile; a smile of friendship and understanding and sympathy. Nothing more. But Brett, busy with a batch of culture he was incubating, glanced up and saw the smile, and because subconsciously he was jealous of Andrew McNeil's friendship with Linda and because he himself loved her, he read more into it than was actually there. He saw it as a secret, significant smile, full of meaning—one which spoke volumes between them, one which shut him out, one which marked the dividing line between himself and Linda and reminded him that to hope for her love was to aspire too high. Last night was best forgotten . . .

He locked the incubator and went back to

his worktable, turning his back upon them. But not before he had heard Linda say: "You're just the man I want to see!"

Just the man she wanted to see. The only man? Why not? It was common gossip in the hospital that the McNeil-Powell marriage was an accepted thing. What difference did age make? It was position which counted with people like the Powells. Linda was, after all, their daughter, brought up with certain accepted standards, standards she would never be able to reject. Briskly, almost savagely, Brett set a distillation in motion. He was glad when the hissing and bubbling drowned the conversation at the end of the room. He did not want to hear, did not want to listen to Linda's voice, speaking confidentially to Andrew McNeil. Work was again his refuge. He was safe in his cold, scientific world where no human emotion could disturb him.

But one thing he did overhear, as the surgeon turned to go.

'Why not lunch with me, Linda? We'd have more time to talk.'

Brett observed how her face lit up—lit up with a smile which tore at his own heart. Lit up with radiance and even gratitude!

'I'd love to, Andrew!'

Andrew McNeil said lightly: 'The pleasure will be mine, Linda—you know that.'

He spoke in the manner of an older brother, but he didn't feel like one, Brett knew. A sudden spasm of envy and hatred and sheer physical pain stabbed his heart. Lunching with Andrew McNeil—successful, self-assured, distinguished—she would forget that hour spent in a humble restaurant with a young man who talked about his homely, middle-class background. Or, if she remembered, it would mean nothing more to her than a brief insight into another world.

Andrew McNeil paused beside Brett and said amiably: 'I really came to see you, Rogers, about that cerebral tumor—' and Brett produced his report at once, losing his self-consciousness, forgetting his shyness as he discussed his work. In the field of medical research he was completely at home and, listening to him, McNeil thought: 'I was right about this man—he is brilliant. No wonder Linda is proud to work for him!'

After he had gone, Brett thought: I wish I didn't like McNeil so much. But he is one of the best. And she deserves only the best . . .

It was some time before he spoke to Linda again. They worked in silence throughout the morning and when, at the end of it, it became necessary for Brett to discuss the afternoon's work, she sensed a withdrawal in his manner, a frigidness which chilled her. How she was ever going to penetrate the proud recesses of this man's heart she really did not know.

CHAPTER SIX

Andrew was awaiting her in the lounge of Rockport's most fashionable hotel. Linda noted idly, as she walked down the center of the green-and-gold lounge amid massed flowers and vast, gilt-framed mirrors and ornate Louis Quinze chairs, that many of her one-time schoolfellows frequented the Royal at this hour. They were all daughters of local merchants, or prominent professional families, or 'high-up' naval officials, and they all had one thing in common—too much money and too much time on their hands.

Shirley Travers, for instance—there she was, seated on a high stool at the red-topped American bar, amidst a cohort of young men, one of whom was the handsome, impecunious Keith Saunders. And seeing Keith reminded Linda of the real object of her visit here, the motive for her lunch. Meg Watling. Pretty, pathetic little Meg whom she wanted so badly to help.

She quickened her steps as she passed the entrance to the American bar, but Shirley's keen eyes saw her, her sharp voice hailed her, and there was Keith—dispatched like an obedient messenger—to fetch her. 'But you must!' he insisted. 'There's time for a cocktail before lunch, Linda, and no one ever sees you these days—' His hand was firm and compelling beneath her elbow, propelling her into the gay, chattering bar. Before she had time to think of an excuse she found herself seated upon a high stool beside Shirley, with a dry Martini in front of her.

Shirley Travers was certainly pretty. She had wide, innocent blue eyes—eyes which missed nothing. She had a pouting, full-lipped mouth—a fretful, pleading little mouth which could, nevertheless, be surprisingly spiteful. Now her voice purred:

'Darling—wonderful to see you! You're so elusive these days! Where do you hide yourself?'

'Mostly in the lab. The rest of the time in the nurses' home.'

Shirley suppressed a mock shudder and, turning to her court, announced: 'Linda's a career woman, you know. Life is very real and earnest to her, I assure you!' She sighed and said with exaggerated emphasis: 'I've always envied you your brains, darling!'

Keith Saunders' hand stretched in front of Linda again, pushing her empty glass across the bar while he commanded the bartender, peremptorily, to refill it. Linda observed, with dislike, that his hand was short and square, the fingers thick and blunt and brutal. Rather a surprising hand in a young man so polished and charming.

'Not another for me,' she said. 'I have an

appointment for lunch—'

Shirley raised arched eyebrows.

'And *I* know who with, my dear. The faithful Andrew!'

Linda glanced at her in astonishment. Andrew—faithful? To whom?

Her voice was cool as she answered: 'He is an old friend of the family, Shirley, and I don't want to keep him waiting. Besides, I have to be back at the hospital at two-fifteen . . .'

Shirley waved a negligent hand. 'Surely lunch with the senior visiting surgeon is sufficient excuse to be late? Don't tell me that the big shots at that hospital don't take all the time they like!'

'That is precisely what they don't do,' Linda told her. 'I'm sure Andrew will be as eager as I to get back promptly. He is operating this afternoon.'

'Is that why he wouldn't join us in the bar?' asked someone. 'We tried to persuade him—'

'Very probably. He never drinks before operating.'

'What a virtuous, reliable husband he will make!' sang Shirley.

That seemed so trivial that Linda let it pass. She finished her drink and gathered up her bag and gloves. 'You really must excuse me,' she said.

Andrew, of course, was waiting. He looked tall and distinguished in his well-tailored suit, his hair silver at the temples, his figure lean and well balanced. He held out his long, sensitive hand as he greeted her. 'I hope I haven't kept you waiting,' said Linda, knowing quite well that she had.

'Not too long, anyway,' he smiled. 'A drink before lunch?'

'I have just had one.'

'Then we'll go straight in—I've reserved a table over in that far corner. It is quiet and secluded.'

At any other moment Linda would have been glad, but now her first fleeting thought was: *That* will give the gossips something to churn over! But they would find something, anyway... She really was glad of the quiet and seclusion, for to talk in the center of the Royal Grill was always trying. Following the deferential head waiter, Linda fumed over Shirley's stupid comment. Herself and Andrew McNeil! Whoever thought up anything so ridiculous? Why, she had known Andrew since her childhood, when he was staff surgeon at the Royal Nelson, junior to her own father! He was like an uncle to her, or an elder brother at the most. The idea of having him as a husband was so ludicrous that she wanted to laugh aloud. And how long had the idea been bandied about Rockport? And how amazing it was, she thought with wry humor, that the subject of such gossip should always be the last to hear of it! She wondered what Andrew would say if he heard, and knew that he would laugh as greatly as she did herself.

'And now,' he said gently as they turned their attention to melon, 'what is this problem on which you want advice?'

'How to restore a pretty girl's face.'

'You mean—?'

'It is scarred on one side. A car accident about a year ago.'

'Badly scarred?'

'Pretty badly.'

'It should have been attended to at once.'

'It was, as far as possible—which means, as far as funds would allow—but no further. It is tragic, Andrew. Can't you help?'

'Not unless I see the girl.'

'I can't ask her to come to see you—she wouldn't, unless she could afford to pay. And I don't think she would accept charity of any kind from me, although I'd willingly stand the cost of any treatment necessary.'

'But if she won't come to see me—'

'*You* can see *her*!' finished Linda. 'At any time. She's in Cunningham Ward. A new student nurse. Couldn't you take a look at her when you visit your cases?'

'I don't see why not. I have to go down there this afternoon, after I finish in the theatre. I want to examine young Richard Herrick—he's in a private ward attached to Cunningham.'

'Not now, I believe. I heard Nurse Humphrey say he'd been moved on to the general.'

Andrew looked surprised.

'At whose orders?'

'The new house physician's—backed by Matron. It created quite a stir.'

'It would,' smiled Andrew, 'but so long as it has Matron's approval, it has mine.'

'You like her, don't you?'

'She's a wonderful woman.'

'Wonderful because she is still human.'

'But to get back to this nurse—what is her name?'

'Watling. Meg Watling. I feel sure it isn't too late for something to be done.'

'I'm not saying it will be too late, but it will take longer, of course. And I'll have to examine her—partially, at any rate. I'm not a skin specialist, you know, or a plastic surgeon, but if I thought something could be done I would pass her on to the right man.'

'Simon Wardour, by any chance? Oh, Andrew, if you could it would be wonderful! He's the finest man in that line, isn't he?'

'The best in England. Is this girl on duty this afternoon?'

'She is. I know, because I share a room with her at the home—she and Janet Humphrey and myself.'

'Humphrey? You mean Nurse Humphrey who is going to marry Bailey? Somehow, I never imagined him to be a marrying man . . .'

'I imagined less that Janet would marry *him*! But there it is. Not that I think it will remain

51

there, somehow . . .'

'Why not?'

Linda smiled and shrugged. She wanted to say: 'Because of an Irish doctor with a roguish eye—and obvious determination,' but thought better of it. There were enough gossips in Rockport without swelling their ranks. Not that Andrew would pass it on—he was too absorbed in his work to spare time for gossip. Nice Andrew. Kind Andrew. She was glad that she had lunched with him, glad she had made this opportunity to broach the subject of Meg Watling. If any man would help the girl, Andrew McNeil would. It had been an hour well spent, she thought, as they passed through the Grill Room again.

But this time Linda was conscious of watchful eyes. She had never observed this curiosity before—perhaps because the idea of a romance between herself and Andrew McNeil had never occurred to her. Who started the ridiculous rumor, anyway? She knew a swift thankfulness because Brett kept himself detached from the social circle of Rockport. It would have been too awful if he had the same idea . . .

CHAPTER SEVEN

Powdering her nose in the discreetly lighted ladies' room, Linda became aware of a familiar perfume and turned to see her mother bearing down upon her.

'Linda, dear child! You didn't let me know you were lunching here!'

'I didn't know myself, until this morning.'

Linda kissed the carefully powdered cheek. Her mother was wrapped in furs, like a stout butterfly in a chrysalis. Everything about Elizabeth Powell was well preserved. She had never known struggle, never had to work. Her chatter came from a mind encased in cotton wool.

'Thank goodness you do eat a good meal sometimes, my dear, instead of ruining your digestion in that awful staff cafeteria!'

Linda smiled and carefully applied her lipstick.

'You should visit the cafeteria one day, Mother. You'd get a surprise.'

They walked down the stairs together.

'Daddy here?'

'No, darling. You know, I can never get your father to lunch at the Royal. Likes to lunch at home, he says, where he can hear himself think! So unsociable of him! I've been lunching with your aunt.'

'Not Ethel?' groaned Linda.

'But why not, dear? She is always so bright and has lots of news. You should have joined us—but I didn't see you in the dining-room,' she remembered, casting a bright, curious glance at her daughter.

'We were in the Grill.'

'We?'

'Andrew and I.'

'Andrew!' Elizabeth's eyes brightened. They looked like two bright currants in a lump of dough. I wish Mother wouldn't use so much make-up, thought Linda affectionately. It makes her look older, not younger . . . All the same, she was a dear, if a little trying at times.

She felt the stout, be-ringed fingers squeeze her own.

'Darling, I'm so glad! I had no idea you and Andrew—'

Linda stood still.

'No idea I and Andrew—what?'

'That you lunch together. You've never *told* me . . .'

'Because we never do.'

'Oh well, there always has to be a beginning,' commented her mother complacently, sailing on down the stairs. Her gratification was obvious. So obvious that a startling thought sent Linda hurrying after her. Surely her own mother could not be responsible for circulating that ridiculous idea?

54

'Mother—wait!'

Linda saw her aunt striding toward them and, panic-stricken, clutched her mother's arm.

'Mother—quickly—tell me before Ethel joins us—'

'Linda, dear, I think you're so unkind to dear Ethel, trying to avoid her always . . . Why do you?'

'Because she talks more and says less than any woman I know. Listen to me, Mother, *please*!'

But it was too late. Her mother's expensive sables were joined by Aunt Ethel's expensive tweeds.

'Ha, Linda!' she boomed. 'Where did you spring from?'

Linda flinched. Somehow, she always expected Aunt Ethel to slap her upon the back.

'From the Grill Room,' said Elizabeth, adding with satisfaction: 'She was lunching with Andrew . . .' She put the world of significance into the statement and Aunt Ethel reacted accordingly.

'In a discreet corner, eh? No wonder we didn't see them, Elizabeth. We weren't meant to!'

Her voice could be heard the length and breadth of the hotel lounge.

Anger surged through Linda in an engulfing tide. She turned upon her heel, not trusting speech.

'Where are you going?' Elizabeth demanded.

'Back to the hospital,' Linda answered abruptly, pausing to kiss her mother's agitated cheek. 'Give my love to Daddy.'

Her mother sighed.

'What you see in that depressing laboratory, I can't think, Linda!'

'Condensing flasks and reagents; serums and test-tubes,' Linda told her, 'and *not* Andrew McNeil. Sorry to disappoint you!'

And she hurried away.

Outside, Andrew waited by his car. He observed two bright spots of color in her cheeks and said: 'You look ruffled, my dear. 'What's wrong?'

'Heated is the word, Andrew. I've just been rude to Aunt Ethel.'

He chuckled.

'Haven't you always wanted to be?'

'Passionately!'

'Confidentially, so have I,' he confessed. They laughed together as the car slid away from the curb and wended its way across Rockport toward the vast, gaunt building of the hospital, standing proudly upon its hill.

Waiting for the elevator to take her up to the laboratory, Linda saw Janet's immaculate white figure disappearing down the corridor to Cunningham Ward. Doctor O'Hara walked beside her. He was looking down at her, a

56

crooked, attractive little smile playing about his lips. And suddenly he caught hold of her left hand and examined it—and said something. Janet snatched her hand away and hurried on, but Shaun merely laughed. Linda could hear his deep, provocative chuckle. She stepped into the elevator and closed the gates thinking: If I didn't love Brett so much, I'd find that chuckle hard to resist . . .

Was that why Janet ran away?

Entering the laboratory, Linda was surprised to find Brett still at work. She said abruptly: 'You haven't lunched!'

He did not look up. She crossed to him and glanced over his shoulder, and he said irritably: 'All right, all right—I haven't eaten! So what? I won't starve. This report on Doctor O'Hara's fractional test meal has to go down at three. He particularly wants it, he says. Came in just after you'd left.'

'I'm sorry.'

'Why?'

She shrugged.

'You make me feel I should not have lunched, either . . .'

'Nonsense. But it would have been a good idea to get back on time.'

He was in a mood. A deep, black mood which clouded the laboratory like a fog. Any other girl, thought Linda, would lose her temper in return—but I can't. Because I feel sorry for him. Because he is unhappy. Because

I love him . . .

And, loving him, she understood so well how he felt, how, in his loneliness, he resorted to ill-temper and impatience to cover his pain. He *was* a lonely man—how lonely she had never realized until last night. Until he told her of his childhood and the noisy, happy family among whom he felt isolated and alone. How could a clear scientific mind like his find companionship there? And now, grown up and successful, he lived a solitary life in his bachelor flat, believing he needed, and wanted, nothing more.

She said evenly: 'I'm sorry I am late—but only ten minutes. I'll make up the time at the end of the day.'

He answered without looking at her: 'Rot. I'm just in a foul temper. Take no notice . . .'

She smiled at his averted head and, crossing to her locker, took out her white coverall. From the high window of the laboratory she saw Meg Watling's neat figure crossing the courtyard toward the dispensary. Three girls in white, thought Linda—that's us. Janet, myself and Meg. And all at the mercy of love . . . Meg hurt by the selfish Keith; myself by Brett; and Janet—how could the cold, frigid love of a man like Augustus Bailey bring her anything but heartache? Suddenly depressed, Linda walked out of the laboratory and down the stairs to the cafeteria.

When she returned Brett said abruptly:

'Where have you been?' and without a word she placed before him the sandwiches and coffee she had brought. Her mouth wore an unaccustomed droop—tiredness, or disappointment? he wondered. She had gone to lunch with McNeil eagerly enough.

She crossed the room to her own table—cleared, as always for action.

Brett mumbled: 'Thank you for this—' but she made no answer. He watched her for a while. 'What's that you're working on?' he asked.

'Blood count for Rodney Ward. That leukemia you told me to start.'

'Good.'

Silence. At the far end of the room a guinea pig scratched about in its cage. Into a deep sink—Brett's sink, beside his scrubbed bench—water dripped with monotonous regularity. In the sink was an enamel bowl containing a lump of tissue submerged in spirit. Across the room another distillation bubbled, and the hissing blue flame spluttered beneath the sand bath. These were the only sounds in the white-tiled room, with its rows of glass bottles and specimen jars.

Brett said quietly: 'Enjoy your lunch?'

'Very much.'

'McNeil's a nice chap.'

'I'm very fond of him.'

He wanted to say: 'How fond?' but the words stuck in his throat. He washed them

59

away with a gulp of scalding coffee.

'Of course I've known him all my life,' Linda continued.

A good basis for marriage, he thought bitterly—lifelong friendship. No wild and sudden love, but a deep, quiet affection which could bring no storms in its wake. He experienced a sudden rush of longing which flooded his heart in an almost terrifying surge. He wanted to go to her and gather her in his arms and cling to her—desperately, angrily. He wanted to shout defiance at all the men who had ever loved her, or who would ever dare to love her. He turned swiftly back to his desk, and Linda said calmly: 'You've forgotten your sandwiches . . .'

'I'm not hungry.'

She covered them with a plate and put them away in a cupboard, saying: 'Perhaps later.' She did not fuss, or nag him, or push food at him like an anxious mother. She had a wonderful ability for minding her own business, yet looking after him at the same time. He realized that during the two years she had worked for him she had unobtrusively taken care of him, too. He wanted to put his face down on the table and cover it with his hands. Instead, he quietly and deliberately continued with his work. And once more the gulf was between them, stretching endlessly and eternally. A gulf neither could bridge.

CHAPTER EIGHT

Going on afternoon duty, Janet met Doctor O'Hara. It was surprising how frequently she seemed to bump into him. His predecessor, Doctor Heron, had never been so conscientious, she reflected; he had never found it necessary to visit the wards more than twice daily, apart from emergencies. But Doctor O'Hara seemed, all too frequently, to find it necessary to look in at Cunningham.

He waylaid her with his teasing, provocative smile.

'Eaten a good lunch, Nurse? You must build up your strength, you know, if you are going to undertake the full time job of being Mrs. Augustus!'

'Phillip,' she murmured automatically.

'Do you really think Phillip suits him better?' he said reflectively. 'I don't. I actually think Augustus was born to be Augustus. Do you think his parents knew that, too? Do you think his mother, with her first loving glance, visualized the pale-rimmed specs and the stiff white collar—not to mention the black jacket and striped trousers? Or perhaps he inherited them? Perhaps he comes of a long line of black jackets!'

Indignantly she walked on, determined to ignore him, but he caught hold of her hand—

chuckling in that infuriating way of his—and looked at it. 'With the right kind of ring,' he said, 'your hand would be beautiful. Do you know what stone *I* would choose for you?'

Despite her better judgment, she asked: 'And what stone would you choose, Doctor?' But she tried to keep her voice frigid.

'A ruby. Warm and glowing and alive. Like yourself—or as you could be.'

She snatched her hand away and hurried ahead. She heard his deep, gentle laugh following her down the corridor. It mocked and scorned her. It taunted her. It made her want to cry—and to laugh, too. Strange, the effect this aggravating young doctor was having upon her . . . Ignore him as she might, she found it impossible to forget him. He was too vital. Too forceful. Too dominating.

And she did not like the dominating type. She did not like a pair of eyes which saw through her and laughed at what they saw. She did not like a voice with a soft Irish brogue which ridiculed her marriage to a fine, steady, upright man. Why, she thought angrily, Phillip is worth a hundred Shaun O'Haras! And although she was at pains to tell him so—in her words, her glances, her indignation and contempt—it seemed to make no impression at all.

Determinedly, she thrust the thought of him aside. There were two unexpected abdominals to prepare for this afternoon and only an hour in which to do them.

Janet hurried on to the ward to give the first patient his pre-operational injection. He looked at her anxiously and she gave him her warm, reassuring smile, forgetting, in the immediate urgency of her work, the disturbing Shaun O'Hara.

She saw Meg Watling leaving Richard Herrick's bedside. She had been feeding him from a drinking-cup, mothering him like the tender-hearted creature she was. The pathos of the little student touched Janet's heart anew. Life had been cruel to cheat her of so much. This girl should be mothering her own brood, not redirecting her maternal instincts to patients who would forget her as soon as they left the hospital.

Yet as those bandaged eyes turned instinctively to follow Meg down the ward, something in Janet's consciousness stirred, and questioned, and wondered.

Janet took hold of the patient's arm, cleansed the area for injection and deftly inserted the hypodermic. 'This will make you feel better,' she said reassuringly. 'I'll even wager you will be asleep before we want you to be!' The shot was to lull the nerves and produce a soothing drowsiness before the anesthetic. She gave his shoulder a reassuring pat, replaced her hypodermic in its sterilized tray and carried it out to the ward kitchen.

And came face to face, once more, with

Shaun O'Hara.

She stood still and took a deep breath and, seeing her reaction, he laughed. 'You do get around, don't you, Doctor?' she said scathingly, and handed the enamel surgical tray to Meg. 'You know what to do with it, Nurse?' she questioned formally, and received the girl's confident nod. Meg was shaping up well, thought Janet, turning back to Doctor O'Hara and saying briskly: 'Do you require anything in this kitchen, Doctor?'

'I hoped there might be an after-lunch cup of tea available—a luxury we don't get in the residents' dining-room. Am I out of luck?'

'You *are*, I am afraid. Four o'clock is the hour.'

'Thanks, Nurse—I'll remember. Meanwhile, Sister had better be notified that Mr. McNeil is coming down to examine young Herrick's eyes after he has finished operating. He had a word with me before going to the theatre.'

'He wanted to know, I expect, why you moved the patient?'

'He did. And I told him.'

'Any opposition?'

'None. The fact that Matron supported me seemed to clinch it.'

'It would. He thinks highly of her.'

'She seems a grand person.'

'She is grand.'

The door swung open and Sister Marlow appeared, with Meg following.

'Mr. McNeil is coming down to examine Richard Herrick, Sister,' Janet said.

'I know, I know,' Sister snapped. 'Doctor O'Hara has already told me that.' She moved briskly toward the medicine cabinet, not seeing the guilty smile Shaun gave Janet, nor Janet's raised eyebrows which questioned whether it had *really* been necessary to bring the news to the ward kitchen, too. He swung his long, lean figure toward the door, glanced over his shoulder again and, waving an airy hand, departed.

Sister Marlow said briskly: 'I'll take a look at young Herrick's dressing myself, right away. Put the screens round his bed at once, please.' And Meg, her heart thumping in a wild, unaccountable fashion, departed to obey.

Walking down the long room, she saw Richard's dark head, his thick black hair curling above his forehead, his brow strong and tanned above the white bandage, and the deep thudding of her heart lessened to a tender rhythm. Something about the stoic acceptance of his affliction touched her deeply—something about that suggestion of leashed strength, of vigor bound and restricted, moved her to a strange and pitying humility. Who am I, she thought, to rebel against fate when I can see without stumbling, move without aid, when my whole life is not threatened by eternal darkness? Nurse Humphrey had told her that the chance of

65

Richard's ever seeing again was slim. Slim, but not hopeless. Would Mr. McNeil give his verdict this afternoon? Would he decide today whether it was safe to operate?

Richard knew her footfall and turned his head eagerly, wondering if she would pass, or whether she would pause and greet him in her soft, gentle voice. He hoped she would. How light her footstep was! Youthful and alive, like herself. The outline of her features, which he had traced with such intense curiosity, was etched upon his mind so vividly that he could visualize her face. And he knew that it was beautiful.

The footsteps paused, as he had hoped they would, and then came the sound of castors revolving upon the polished floor. He knew what that meant. She was wheeling screens toward his bed, making a barrier between it and the next. To conceal himself, or his neighbor? He listened again, intently, but it was hard to tell whether the second screen was placed at his own foot.

'Meg—'

'Nurse!' she corrected with mock severity.

'Are those screens for me?'

'Yes, Mr. Herrick.'

'Richard, please!'

'Richard,' she repeated softly.

'Are they for me?' he insisted.

'Yes,' she told him and, erecting the second screen, was enclosed with him in a private

66

world of their own, for Richard's bed was the last in the ward, near the wall. He held out his hand and, without hesitation, she took it.

'What does it mean, Meg?'

'That Mr. McNeil is coming to examine you.'

'To pass his verdict?'

'That remains to be seen.'

'You honestly don't know?'

'If I did, I would tell you, Richard.'

'You would—I know you would.' His grasp tightened. 'Bless you, Meg. And thank God you have come . . .'

They remained together, for one brief, exquisite moment, before the sound of Sister Marlow's firm footsteps echoed in the ward. 'You'll be here?' Richard whispered urgently, and an answering pressure on his fingers gave him the assurance he sought. And, quite suddenly, he was no longer afraid. In the darkened recesses of his mind he had been afraid for quite a long time; afraid ever since he realized the possibility ahead. They hadn't told him—he knew already. When the doctors and the nurses had spoken so brightly and encouragingly, he had known they did so to mask the truth. But Andrew McNeil had not masked it—he had told him, man to man, that the future was uncertain and that all he could promise was to do his best for him. And he had taken the news, as McNeil had known he would, with characteristic quietness.

But in his heart Richard had been shaken, stunned. In the whole of his young, active life he had never known illness of any kind and had certainly never contemplated the possibility of blindness. How he would take it when the time came, he did not know. *If* the time came . . . If, at the end, he remained in darkness. But now, he thought as he lay there, as Sister Marlow—with cold but kindly efficiency—attended to his dressing, *now* I believe I do. With someone like Meg, I could face anything.

Sister said quietly: 'You know Mr. McNeil is coming to see you?'

'Yes, Sister.'

She touched his arm briefly. It was a kindly touch, but not the same as Meg's. Nor was her voice so infinitely gentle, so sweet to his ears as she said: 'You can have complete trust, complete confidence in Mr. McNeil, you know.'

'I have, Sister.'

He smiled, and little dreamed how her heart, trained into frigidity after years of hospital life, stirred at the sight of that smile. He had a nice mouth, she thought. Firm and humorous, generous and brave. And it parted upon strong white teeth. A nice boy, a handsome boy . . .

She turned away briskly, aware of an unaccountable lump in her throat. If she had not dedicated herself to nursing, she might have had a son like this. There had been a young doctor, years ago—but he had been penniless, and she had been ambitious. More fool I! she thought bitterly. I should have gone with him to that remote little provincial town where he was taking over his father's struggling practice, but I was too great a coward. I wanted security and independence—and I've got both, with loneliness thrown in for good measure.

Nurse Humphrey was standing beside her. A nice girl. A good nurse. Going to marry that pedantic man, Bailey. Couldn't be a love match, it just couldn't! She said abruptly: 'I want a word with you, Nurse . . .' and stepped beyond the screen. Richard Herrick's voice said swiftly: 'Could I have fresh water, please? Perhaps you could send Nurse Watling with it?' Janet smiled suddenly. There was understanding in her voice as she answered: 'Of course I will!'

'I said I wanted a word with you, Nurse!' Sister Marlow repeated, and Janet hurried down the ward after her. Outside the door they met Meg. 'Ah, there you are,' Janet said. 'Please give the patient fresh water, or a cup of tea might be a better idea. It will pep him up before his examination.'

A look of happiness came to Meg's eyes—and, quite suddenly, Janet was aware of a deep and aching envy.

There was a little room at the end of the

69

corridor which Sister Marlow used as an office. And it was here she led Janet, to the girl's surprise and inner apprehension.

When they were alone, Sister said: 'A pity about that boy. You know there *is* a possibility . . .?'

'Yes, Sister. But Mr. McNeil is a brilliant surgeon.'

'Very brilliant,' Sister agreed absently. She looked at Janet as if she had something else on her mind, something she wanted to say. 'I hear you are going to be married?' she added suddenly.

'Why—yes, Sister.'

Sister Marlow's firmly controlled mouth relaxed a little.

'News travels fast in a hospital, Nurse. I congratulate you, of course, although I really think Mr. Bailey is the one to be congratulated.'

She spoke in jerks, nervous and self-conscious when it came to personal discussions with her juniors. Sister Marlow, Janet realized, was only self-confident when issuing orders. Suddenly her heart was filled with a deep and profound pity for the cold, dried-up creature. Beneath that starched apron a heart had once stirred—was it still capable of feeling anything greater than a professional pride in her work?

'I wanted to say, Nurse, that I hope you will be very happy—'

'Thank you, Sister,' said Janet, oddly

touched.

'You are quite sure, I suppose?'

'Sure, Sister? Of course.'

The older woman looked at her anxiously, and Janet marvelled at what she saw. That caustic, sour, cold Sister Marlow should reveal anxiety was incredible. She saw a flush of embarrassment flood the thin, lined face and realized that the woman struggled against an overwhelming shyness.

'I only wondered—wanted you to be happy, Nurse. Really happy. You've been a good and loyal worker all these years. I haven't always been kind, I know . . .'

'Oh, please, Sister! You're one of the finest Sisters the hospital has ever had!'

'Which means I am grim and forbidding and efficient.' Sister Marlow gave a nervous laugh. 'Well, I *am* all those things. Because I've lived for work and nothing else. I've steeled myself against temptations which I regarded as weaknesses—against love—' Coming from her thin, pale lips, the word sounded incongruous and she knew it, for she gave an embarrassed laugh and finished: 'Oh yes, even I once knew it! Even I could have married, long ago . . .'

Janet swallowed. She wanted to cry, which was ridiculous, of course. Never in all her years at the hospital had she seen Sister Marlow relax, never had the stern, gaunt woman revealed even a crack in her veneer of efficiency—yet now, quite suddenly, the walls

71

of her reserve crumbled and out poured all the pent-up longing which she had held in check.

'Make quite, *quite* sure, Janet!' she cried, using the girl's first name spontaneously. Again the self-conscious, nervous little laugh. 'That sounds funny, I know, coming from me—but although I've never married, I do know this: There is only one reason for doing so, only one thing that can make it really worth while. And *they* have discovered it—'

'They?' echoed Janet in a whisper.

'Those two. That boy and girl—the child with the scarred face and the blind boy. If you love like that, if a man can awaken in you that almost unearthly radiance, then you love him, Nurse Humphrey—or else—you don't.'

There was silence in the little room. Sister Marlow's small desk clock, in its neat leather case, ticked loudly. Janet turned toward the door, groped for the handle, and stumbled out into the corridor. As usual, the ward kitchen was her only refuge, and she pushed the swinging door with shaking hands. She thought: I must take no notice . . . I must forget every word she said . . .

CHAPTER NINE

The senior visiting surgeon looked down at Richard Herrick and said: 'I'm going to be

72

frank with you, Herrick. You want me to be, I think.'

The dressing had been replaced, the examination was over, and now, thought Richard with relief, he was to hear the verdict. To operate or not to operate, that was the question, he quoted with an inner smile. Well, whatever was to come, whatever he was to hear, he could take it—now. Strange, how a person could transform one's life like an unexpected ray of sunshine filtering through gloom, turning night into day and despair into hope. There was something about Meg's presence, about her voice, about her quiet movements and gentle touch which had told Richard, at once, that she understood, that she knew what he was suffering, that she did not sympathize as the kindly, competent nursing staff sympathized, but could actually comprehend his anguish. Which was amazing in one so young.

He had touched her hand, briefly, before Andrew McNeil approached his bed. She whispered: 'Good luck!'

'You'll be here, Meg?'

'Not at the examination, Richard, but nearby. As near as I can get. And with you all the time in my mind.'

'I hoped you were going to say: "In my heart . . ."' He caught her hand and held it, whispering urgently: 'Say it, please, Meg!'

'In my heart,' she echoed softly.

Unexpectedly, she stooped and kissed him. And then she was gone. But the touch of her lips lingered upon his own. All the time Andrew McNeil stooped above him, Richard felt the soft, gentle warmth of Meg's kiss, like the lingering melody of a well-loved tune.

So he smiled at Andrew McNeil and said: 'Be as frank as you like. That is what I want.'

'Very well, then. You know what your trouble is—a damaged retina. A small tear, or rent, in the surface. Not a common affliction, but it happens now and then to fairly short-sighted people, especially if they ignore the symptoms of near-sightedness, as you have done. This injury was, at one time, considered hopeless unless nature stepped in, as she sometimes did, and healed the tear. Well, we've given nature her chance, with medical aid thrown in, and she hasn't co-operated.'

'You mean there's no hope?'

'Nothing of the sort! In recent years it has been possible to operate successfully in cases of this kind—but not always. A Swiss surgeon named Gonin did it first. I have done it myself. I might do it again—but no surgeon would dare to predict success.'

'I understand. It is touch and go—is that what you mean?'

'Almost. And I would never insist upon the operation without the patient's consent.'

'What sort of a job is it?' Richard asked curiously.

'One might almost call it a welding job, Herrick. You see, when a small rent like this occurs, the strain of focusing the eye forces the liquid of the eyeball through the tear, and eventually severs the retina from the optical nerves . . .'

'Causing blindness?'

'Yes.'

'And if I don't have the operation, will that happen?'

'Almost certainly.'

'Where does the welding come in?'

'In sealing the torn part. It is done by an electric current.'

'And the chances of success?'

'About even.'

'Then I'll take a chance.'

He heard Andrew McNeil give a short, satisfied sigh.

'Good. I thought you would.'

The surgeon's hand rested briefly upon his shoulder before, with a smile, he went away.

Leaving the ward, Andrew came face to face with Meg. He had been aware of a nurse hovering in the background, but had been too intent upon his patient to notice her consciously. Now, however, he observed the pretty, scarred face and his promise to Linda leapt into his mind. As the girl stepped aside to let him pass he paused and looked at her, observing the sensitive tide of color which flooded her cheek and the nervous clenching and unclenching of her hands. She stood with her arms behind her, believing no one noticed that revealing gesture, but McNeil's professional mind missed nothing.

He smiled at her. 'You're new, aren't you?' he asked.

The student nurse swallowed and said: 'Yes, sir.' She was aware of the surgeon's scrutiny and moved uncomfortably beneath it. Andrew had sharp eyes, but not unkind ones.

'Keen on nursing?' he asked, to make conversation, to gain time in which to study the girl's face.

'Very keen, sir.'

'And you like it here?'

'Very much, indeed.'

'And you live at the nurses' home? I hear the girls have quite a good time over there. Got a nice room? One with a view?'

She wondered why he was asking all these questions, but his interest seemed genuinely friendly and Meg responded, as he had hoped she would, animation lighting her young face and moving the muscles of her wounded cheek. He observed that they were almost normally pliable.

'A lovely view, sir. I can see my home.'

'Indeed? And where is that?'

'Up on Ferrers' Mount—right at the top.'

'Show me,' he said, and moved toward the window. She followed him, as he had intended that she should. She stood with the strong sunlight full upon her face, throwing into relief the quality of her wound. At first Meg was unaware of his interest in it, but suddenly she realized that he was paying little heed to the situation of her father's rose gardens and her sensitive hand flew to her cheek, hiding her scar.

Andrew smiled gently. 'Don't hide it,' he said. 'Why should you?'

Her hand fell.

'Does it make you unhappy, child?'

His voice was surprisingly gentle. She had stood in awe of so great a man, but meeting him was not terrifying at all.

He was kind and humane and understanding. It was easy to answer: 'I have grown more accustomed to it now, sir, but yes—it does make me self-conscious.'

'Ever thought of having treatment for it? There are ways and means, you know.' He lifted his hand and touched her cheek, feeling the texture of the wounded skin, assessing the tension of it across her cheekbone. 'I'm not a specialist in that line,' he murmured, 'but I should think something could be done.' He dropped his hand and said abruptly: 'Would you see a specialist if I arranged it for you?'

'Not unless I could meet the expense myself,' she answered quietly, and, recognizing pride when he saw it, Andrew McNeil said no more. Giving her a brief, understanding smile, he went on his way.

Brett was in the laboratory when the house phone rang. Absently, he heard the lab. boy's voice answering it—perkily at first, then with sudden respect.

'Will you hold on, please, sir?' Then: 'Mr. McNeil to speak to you, Miss Powell.'

Brett noticed how eagerly Linda seized the phone. 'Andrew?' she said, her voice quick and excited.

Brett tried not to listen, but failed. Linda's clear voice came to him across the room. He heard the catch in her breath as she listened, and then: 'Oh, Andrew, do you really think so? It would be wonderful—just wonderful, if we could!'

'I don't see why we couldn't help her,' Andrew was saying. 'I took a good look at the child, and her scar is no worse than hundreds I have seen completely cured.'

But this Brett could not hear. Merely Linda's delighted reply.

'Andrew, you're a darling!'

'The question is—how?' Andrew continued. 'I suggested seeing a specialist, but she shied off at once. She's proud—too proud to accept anything which suggests charity. Foolish of her, but there it is. Told me point-blank that unless she could meet the expense herself, she'd have none of it. I thought it wiser not to pursue the

78

subject. Couldn't you and I, together, hatch an idea?'

'With you, Andrew, I could do anything!' Linda laughed in delight. Brett frowned.

'I could, of course, arrange the meeting quite casually, Linda. A cocktail party at my flat, and an invitation to yourself and friend. You could check up on her off duty hours and let me know—then I'd see how Wardour was fixed and choose a date accordingly. You could bring her along. The whole thing could be completely casual—she wouldn't know she was meeting the best plastic surgeon in England, until later.'

Turning, Brett saw Linda's expression. It was radiant. He thought bitterly: I could never make her look like that . . . He turned away again, but Linda's voice reflected the happiness he had seen in her face.

'Oh, make it soon, Andrew! Very soon!'

'I'll do my best, my dear.'

'I'll refuse all dates until I hear from you.'

'Is it as important as that?'

'Yes,' said Linda softly, 'it is as important as that, Andrew.'

Brett could bear no more. He walked briskly from the room and shut the door firmly behind him. Linda looked round, startled by the sudden slam of the door. 'I'd better go,' she said into the phone. 'I don't know if something urgent has come up, but Doctor Rogers seems in a hurry about something—'

79

CHAPTER TEN

Down in Cunningham Ward the evening rush had begun. Janet hurried out to the ward again, trundling her surgical trolley. She was dining with Phillip tonight—a celebration dinner. She was eager to see him, eager to put the hospital behind her for a few hours at least, eager to reassure herself with the sound of his voice and the air of reliability he always conveyed. Sister Marlow's words were best forgotten, and who could help her to forget better than Phillip himself?

'You can help me on my surgical rounds,' she told Meg and, handling the trolley over to her, walked ahead into the ward, saying as she went: 'It won't be pleasant, but it will be interesting. You're prepared for that?'

'Of course, Nurse.'

Janet smiled. Meg was a stoic little creature. And, of course, she had endured a particularly unpleasant wound herself. Janet had forgotten that. Somehow, when one got to know Meg Watling one completely forgot her disfigurement.

Janet went from bed to bed. To the fractured pelvis, the hernia, the gall-bladder and the appendix. To the laparotomy, which had been worse than expected. The poor fellow didn't look too good. An aged seaman, tough and weatherbeaten—had he strength enough to fight this terrible storm? She felt anxious about him and, apparently, so did Doctor O'Hara, for he appeared at that moment and she stood aside to let him examine the patient. The fact that he paid so many visits to the man was significant.

Janet watched Shaun as he stooped above the bed, thinking how different he was when working—serious, intent, it did not seem possible that he could ever be gay. And how gently he handled the patient! How thorough and careful he was! A nurse was moved to admiration by such a doctor, recognizing in him a deep love of his work. Medicine, to Shaun, was not merely a career. It was a sacred trust. It was a religion. It was his life.

Although he had not glanced at her, he knew she was beside him, awaiting his comments or instructions. He said gently: 'Poor fellow—he's having a rough passage, Nurse. But we can help him, you and I . . .' He turned and looked down at her, observing the tender sympathy in her eyes, and he thought then, as he had thought before: this girl was born to nurse, just as she was born to be a woman and to live a woman's life . . .

'He's so game, Doctor. One can help patients like that—they fight with you.'

'How right you are! Luckily, he has a stout heart. There's nothing more we can do for him at the moment. I'll come down to see him during the night.'

'But you will be off duty, Doctor!'

'Off duty?' he echoed. 'Is a doctor ever off duty?'

She was about to say: 'Doctor Heron never visited the patients after his relief took over,' but something made her bite the words back. Doctor O'Hara was not Doctor Heron; nor would he ever become like him. She felt a new respect welling up in her heart—it was nothing more than professional admiration, of course. She was not interested in Shaun O'Hara as a man, merely as a doctor whom she had to assist.

As she swabbed and sterilized and re-bandaged, Janet found herself looking down the years ahead. They stretched before her in a long, straight road—a highly respectable and conventional road, along which she walked as Janet Bailey, dignified and quiet. There was no turning off the road, no variation; in fact, it looked almost monotonous. She had to jerk her mind away from it. What did she want, anyway? She had known excitement enough in this hospital life—she should be looking forward to a little peace and quiet; to a comfortable, secure existence; to a life of domestic happiness. Why, therefore, did the picture seem a little dull? She had always declared her readiness to abandon this life of underpaid drudgery, and now she was about to do so.

She passed on to the next bed. It was Richard Herrick's. He sat propped up against his pillows, the picture of patience, as usual. But now there was a curve of contentment about his mouth. At her approach he turned his head. 'That you, Nurse?' he asked, and his voice betrayed a note of eagerness.

'It is—but not the nurse you want!'

He laughed.

'Is that the dressing trolley you're trundling round the ward?'

'Yes—but *I* am not trundling it.' She gave a gentle laugh. 'Nurse Watling is.'

She could almost feel the boy's pleasure. She took the trolley from Meg and said: 'I'll carry on—I've attended to the worst cases. You can start preparing the patients for dinner—starting with this bed.'

She left the pair alone. When she wheeled the surgical trolley out of the ward she saw Meg giving Richard a drink of water. He was trying to reach her hand, but, diligently, she evaded his touch. Janet guessed she only did so because, professionally, she was compelled to.

Abruptly, Janet turned her back. Was it really true, what Sister had said about those two? If so, it was surprisingly lenient of Sister Marlow to pretend to overlook it. One would not have expected such indulgence from her. Why did she do it? Because she pitied them? Because of the boy's blindness and the girl's pathetic disfigurement? Or because, in the lonely recesses of her frigid heart, something stirred in response, something was touched by the radiance in Meg's face whenever she looked upon Richard Herrick? An 'unearthly radiance,' Sister had called it—and Sister had been right.

Had she been right about the rest, as well?

CHAPTER ELEVEN

Phillip frequently chose a quiet, select restaurant just outside Rockport. It had an air of stolid dignity into which he blended well. But tonight, Janet thought, he would surely choose something a little more gay. The Royal, perhaps, since they were celebrating . . .

She dressed with care. Meg lay upon her bed, watching and admiring. 'That's a lovely suit,' she said. 'Grey suits you. And I love the flame color of your blouse. It's gay.' The bright touch was the only relief to Janet's quiet ensemble, and now she matched it with a new lipstick, a little more heavily applied than usual. It emphasized the curve of her generous mouth and, impulsively, Meg said: 'Why don't you always make your mouth up like that? It suits you.'

Janet put her head upon one side, surveying the effect.

'Do you really think so? I always feel what my grandmother used to call A Painted Woman when I use lipstick heavily! But I admit I don't really want to rub any off . . .'

The door swung open and Linda appeared.

'Had a good day?' Janet asked.

'So-so. Brett's been like a bear with a sore head, heaven knows why, and at lunch I bumped into my most detestable aunt. Sometimes I wonder who are the most trying—relatives or pathologists!'

'You know perfectly well that however disgruntled our dear Doctor Rogers might be, you'd find excuses for him.'

'Doesn't everyone?'

'Yes—but I can't think why. He stalks down to the ward looking for clinical material like a big game hunter looking for buffalo—frowning ferociously all the time. I don't think he sees the patients as human beings—merely as guinea pigs.'

Linda protested indignantly: 'He is completely absorbed in his work, and it's lucky for this hospital that he is!'

'Oh, he's clever, I admit. But is he human? You ought to be able to answer that one; you've worked with him long enough.'

'Yes,' said Linda softly, 'he *is* human. Very human, beneath his armor.'

'Armor?' echoed Janet, adjusting her new little hat at what she hoped was the right angle. 'What does he need armor for?'

Carrying soap and towel, Linda made for the door. 'Defense,' she said over her shoulder.

Janet stared.

'*Defense?* Against what?'

'Against the world,' Linda answered, and closed the door behind her.

'What is he like?' Meg asked. 'The pathologist, I mean. I have only seen him from a distance.'

'Well,' reflected Janet, busy with her hat again, 'I'd say he's like a surly bull-dog, but there's something awfully likable about him.'

Meg laughed.

'Lots of people like bull-dogs. I do myself.'

'That goes for Linda, too. The pathological variety. She always leaps to defend Brett Rogers.'

'But why does he have to be defended?'

Janet smiled wryly.

'Everyone has to be, in this hospital, my dear. Or in any hospital, if it comes to that. The medical staff is always pulled to pieces. You'll find out. You'll do it yourself.'

'But not critically. I admire the medical staff. Especially Doctor O'Hara.'

'And why Doctor O'Hara?'

'Because he has been so understanding with Richard.'

'Richard who?' Janet asked absently; she was not really satisfied with this hat. She was beginning to wonder why she had bought it.

'What d'you think of this hat?' she asked Meg abruptly. 'Shall I wear it, or leave it behind?'

'Where are you dining?'

'I hope—the Royal Grill.'

'Then carry it casually in your hand. Your hair is worth showing, and you cover it with a cap all day. It is neat enough and short enough to look smart.'

Off came the hat. Janet glanced at her watch, flicked a comb through her hair and said: 'And does Richard Herrick think a lot of Doctor O'Hara?'

'Of course.'

'Of course?' Janet echoed softly, then turned and looked at the girl. Meg's eyes revealed a glow which, tritely, Janet could only describe as 'melting.' It certainly melted her own heart, for she went over to the girl, touched her on the shoulder and said hesitantly: 'Meg, would you hate me if I offered advice?'

'What sort?'

'About caring too much for one's patients— oh, don't misunderstand!' she cried, and hurried on: 'I've done it myself, so often! Especially when I first began nursing. But however devoted they become—and, believe me, some patients do become devoted to the nurses!—they soon forget, once they leave the hospital. That is as it should be, of course. It proves that we've done our job, made them thoroughly well, but . . .'

'But as to our loving them,' said Meg softly, 'that would be foolishness?'

'I'm afraid so, Meg.'

'And you are right. I know that.' Meg stood up briskly. 'I know what you are thinking, Nurse—'

'Janet, off duty.'

'I know what you are thinking, Janet, but please don't worry. If I can help patients by giving them affection when they need it, what harm is there in that?'

'No harm at all, so long as you can turn it off, like a tap. But you can't. You're not made that way, Meg. Oh, my dear, don't make the fatal mistake of allowing your heart to take part in your nursing! It must, up to a point, of course—the point of sympathy and understanding, but not caring . . .'

Meg regarded her steadily.

'You mean, don't you, that you're afraid I shall fall in love with Richard Herrick?'

Janet was silent. If Sister was right, the child had already done so. And he with her. But would it last? Would Meg be hurt in the end? One man had done that already. And there was a wide gulf between the rose gardens on Ferrers' Mount and the home of Sir Christopher Herrick.

She said impulsively: 'Forgive me, Meg! You should tell me to mind my own business . . .'

'But it is your business. I'm your student nurse; the way I conduct myself in the ward is your concern.' She smiled swiftly. 'Don't think I hate you for what you have said. How could I? But please don't worry, either. I have my own solution.'

But what that solution was, Janet was never to know, for at that moment Linda returned, demanding gaily: 'And where are you going, Nurse Humphrey, all dressed to kill?'

'To dine with Phillip.'

'A celebration? I'm glad. I hope you have a wonderful evening. What about you, Meg? Going out, or spending a truly spinster evening with me?'

'A spinster evening it is,' Meg smiled. She did not add that it was a long time since a man had wanted to take her out and that she very much doubted whether one would ever do so again. She had seen Keith shrink from her— she had vowed then that never would she expose herself to such another moment.

'Good!' cried Linda, zipping her model housecoat. It was a gay affair in striped taffeta. 'What's the verdict about Herrick?' she asked. 'To be, or not to be?'

'To be. Scheduled for Thursday, at ten.'

Janet was aware of Meg's sudden stillness.

'Any hope for the poor boy?' asked Linda.

'Fifty-fifty, Sister tells me. It will be an exciting operation. I wish I could see it.'

'From all the hum and gossip about it,' commented Linda, 'I gather it is rather unique. I've tried to get Andrew McNeil to talk about it, without success. He never will talk shop!'

'Unusual, for a surgeon,' said Janet. 'Generally, they love to.'

'Talk about it now!' begged Meg. 'I want to hear about this operation.'

'I don't know much about it,' said Janet, 'except that the stage is set in reverse, so to speak. Light reduced to a minimum; one solitary beam focused on the retina, nothing more. Aprons and masks and caps are black, instead of white—'

'But why?'

'To counteract any dazzle.'

'Go on!' pleaded Meg.

'It's a highly delicate operation, of course. There will be picked students from the London medical schools to watch, although how they will see anything through their glass screen when the theatre is practically in darkness, I can't imagine.'

'And after it,' whispered Meg, 'will the patient be able to see?'

'We don't know,' Janet repeated. 'We hope so, Meg.'

In her heart, Meg whispered: So do I! Dear God, so do I! For Richard's sake, but not my own . . .

CHAPTER TWELVE

Despite Janet's hope that Phillip would choose the Royal Grill, his neat black car took them, as usual, to the 'quiet little place out of town.' She stifled a twinge of disappointment. After all, it was up to her to suggest dining elsewhere—she had no doubt at all that Phillip would have agreed. It just didn't occur to him that she might prefer a change.

They had their usual table and Phillip sat opposite her, as always, immaculate in his well-tailored suit, exuding his usual air of well-being. Janet had always admired Phillip's grooming, and it occurred to her now that she had never seen him untidy, never known him to relax in old tweeds or whipcords as, she suspected, Shaun O'Hara would, off duty. A day in the country produced an equally well-tailored Phillip in good Harris tweeds and well-polished brogues; he wore spotless flannels for tennis and shirts worthy of a soap flake advertisement; when dancing, his evening clothes were always the best on the floor. And whatever he wore, wherever they went, he carried with him that pleasant odor of good soap and expensive hair tonic. Hygienically, the man was perfect.

He ordered for her, as usual. Phillip knew the correct wines to order for each course and it had become her habit to leave it all to him. Janet had never seen him wash down a meal with a pint of beer. He had more respect, he claimed, both for good food and his digestion.

If the sneaking fear that he might some day become a gourmand ever assailed her, Janet quelled it loyally. There was, she insisted, a difference between appreciation of good fare—and greed.

When he had ordered, Phillip laid aside the menu and gave Janet his attention. He extended his hand and took hers. They were well secluded in their corner, otherwise she knew, he would have been more discreet. Phillip was never demonstrative in public. Even in private, he was admirably controlled.

'Darling,' he said, 'I have something for you—'

'What is it, Phillip?'

'A ring, of course.'

'A ring!'

'You sound surprised, my dear.' He smiled indulgently. 'It is customary, you know, to present an engagement ring to one's fiancée.'

Janet laughed softly.

'To tell you the truth, Phillip, I hadn't really thought about it . . .'

But that was untrue, she realized. She had thought about it quite a bit since Shaun had said: 'Do you know what stone *I* would choose for you? A ruby—warm and glowing and alive . . .' While she hurried about her duties in the ward she had thought, subconsciously: 'When I wear Phillip's ring I shall feel safe, secure . . .' Safe from what? From another man's mockery?

She had expected, however, that Phillip would let her choose for herself.

He was drawing something from his pocket when the first course arrived, and immediately he thrust it back again. He said: 'It must be a special moment, my dear—uninterrupted. We'll wait, shall we, until we have finished eating?'

'Oh, please, Phillip—no!'

He glanced at his soup. It seemed quite hot; hot enough to wait for a minute or two, at least. 'Oh, very well, darling,' he said indulgently, and placed before her a small, worn jewel box.

'My mother's,' he said fondly. 'It was her engagement ring. She left it to me, for the girl who became my wife . . .'

'What a lovely thought, Phillip!'

She opened the box. Against faded velvet lay a heavy gold ring, set with a large pearl and two small opals. It was charming, but Janet's throat ached unaccountably.

'You do like it, don't you, Janet?'

'Oh, yes, Phillip!' She forced a smile. How could she tell him that the ring, illogically, made her feel sad?

'You don't seem overjoyed, my dear.'

'I'm silly, Phillip—take no notice. It's just

that I've always had a feeling about opals . . .'

'A feeling?' he echoed with a frown.

'They are supposed to be unlucky. And pearls, Phillip—don't they say that pearls in an engagement ring mean tears?'

'Nonsense! How can they? Really, my dear, I had no notion you were so superstitious!'

'Lots of nurses are. We have hunches about wards, and patients, and things like that.'

'Ridiculous!' Phillip frowned his disapproval. His voice became distant. 'Of course, if you don't *like* the ring . . .' He picked up his soup spoon and did not look at her again.

'But I do! Of course I do.'

He smiled his forgiveness.

'And you'll wear it? I must confess, Janet, I would have been very disappointed in you if you had refused. You've always seemed so level-headed to me. Not like other young women, out for all they can get and with their heads full of ideas about romance. Marriage isn't a romantic affair, after all.'

'Isn't it, Phillip?'

'Of course not. It is a practical, down-to-earth arrangement.'

'Arrangement! Oh no, Phillip, not that!'

'What do you want me to say, my dear— whimsical things about love?'

'Why not? You do love me, don't you?'

'Very much, Janet. I think I have always done so, but particularly this last couple of years. You have matured a lot and shed your

94

girlishness. I knew, then, that it was time to marry you.'

'You sound as if you had weighed it up very carefully, like a business proposition!' Janet laughed.

'One must be practical in all things,' said Phillip, without a vestige of a smile. 'In this matter of the ring, for instance—I should have regarded, with some misgiving, your lack of common sense had you expected me to buy a new one when I already possessed a perfectly good and suitable one.'

Janet experienced an alarming impulse to jump to her feet and run. It was inexplicable and almost frightening for, after all, there was a lot in what Phillip said—especially regarding marriage. She wasn't a girl any more—not a very young one, anyway. Not so young as Meg, nor even as young as Linda. In a month or two she would be twenty-nine, and what Phillip had to offer should appeal to a young woman of her age—stability and quiet companionship, affection and security, and, above all, such sound and logical reasoning.

It was nonsensical to allow dreams to intrude . . .

Phillip was saying quietly: 'You know, my dear, that I will always take care of you. I shall be proud when presenting you as my wife . . .'

A smile trembled upon her lips.

'Phillip, you're a dear—and kind.'

A hovering waiter removed their plates. In

his brief absence Phillip took the ring and placed it upon Janet's finger. It was so heavy and so loose that it slipped to one side.

'It will have to be made smaller,' said Janet.

But Phillip was a practical man.

'I'll have a spring inserted,' he said. 'Better than having it cut, I think. Your hand will probably get fatter in middle age.'

Janet bubbled with laughter. Phillip looked at her in surprise. She spluttered: 'I was just visualizing myself as a stout matron!'

'Matrons very often are,' he said solemnly, unable to see the cause for her laughter.

Janet subsided. She said gently: 'Thank you for the ring, Phillip.'

'And thank you, my dear, for doing me the honor of accepting it. You have made me a very happy man, Janet.'

Why did his conversation seem platitudinous? It had never seemed so before. She had never been aware that he talked in clichés. Janet sipped her Moselle, thinking: 'I must snap out of this mood! It just *isn't* the way to feel on an occasion like this . . .'

As she laid her glass down she was aware of a man seating himself at a nearby table, but she paid no attention until Phillip said with a shade of annoyance:

'Of *all* people to come here! And tonight, of all nights! Can't we ever leave the hospital behind us?'

She followed his glance. The man was

Shaun O'Hara.

He lifted his hand in a casual salute. When he smiled his eyes held their customary twinkle. When the wine waiter hovered deferentially, extending his list, Shaun ignored it, ordering a prosaic beer. He wore a tweed jacket and grey flannels and, as usual, his thick black hair fell forward on his brow. In a moment, thought Janet, he will lift his hand and push it back in that impatient way he has. And even as she thought so, he did.

'Why are you smiling?' said Phillip.

'Was I? I wasn't aware of it.'

'Something amusing you? Could it be Doctor O'Hara? I notice the nursing staff do seem to find the man amusing . . .'

'He is coming over.'

Phillip frowned. Janet had never heard him swear. Perhaps if he had been alone he would have done so.

Shaun's attractive Irish voice greeted them. Phillip was polite enough.

'Celebrating?' said Shaun. 'Allow me to congratulate you, Bailey.'

'Thank you.'

'I have already expressed my feelings to Miss Humphrey.'

That was an odd way of putting it, said Phillip's glance. But Janet knew what he meant. She flushed, looking down at her plate, but she was well aware that Shaun's eyes were upon her and when, at last, she was forced to look up again and meet them, she saw that he was observing her ring. The weight of it seemed suddenly greater, and the color of the stones seemed cold.

They chatted affably for a time, but Janet scarcely heeded the conversation. 'I'm getting back early,' Shaun was saying. 'I'm worried about that laparotomy in your ward, Nurse.'

'Hardly your concern,' said Phillip, 'when you're off duty.'

'My patients are my concern whether I am on duty or not,' Shaun told him and, nodding pleasantly, went back to his table.

An awkward silence followed his departure—like the silence after a roll of drums. Shaun O'Hara was like that—forceful, strong, compelling. One was aware of him even when he said little, even when he exchanged nothing but the lightest of courtesies.

To break the awkward moment Janet said: 'He is conscientious about his job.'

'So was Heron before him, my dear.'

'I never saw Doctor Heron come down to the ward after his relief had taken over.'

'Why should he?'

Janet gave a faint shrug.

'No reason—except a personal interest in his cases, of course.'

'O'Hara has only just qualified, my dear. His enthusiasm will wear off.'

'Do you really think so? I hope not. And,

98

somehow, I believe not.'

'He'll have to learn to toe the line. He throws his weight about too much. We don't like that type of doctor at the Royal Rockport. I understand he acted in a very high-handed manner when he moved Sir Christopher Herrick's son to the general ward.'

'He did it with Matron's support and approval. I was there when he consulted her.'

'I imagine he would have done it, even so.'

Janet laughed: 'So do I!'

'You don't approve of this fellow, surely?'

She glanced across at Shaun, observing the deep lines about his mouth and the unexpected tinge of grey at the temples.

'He is rather old to be newly qualified,' she said reflectively, and in some surprise.

'He is thirty-six. The war, I understand, interrupted his studies, as it did with many medical students.'

'I see—'

She was aware of a sudden desire to know more about Shaun O'Hara, to glimpse his background, his boyhood.

They finished their meal in companionable silence; then Phillip took her back to the nurses' home. Before they parted, he kissed her. He did it precisely and neatly, as he did all things, but there was tenderness in his kiss. He held her a moment before releasing her and said softly: 'Thank you again, my dear. I am very proud . . .'

99

Her heart melted. She touched his cheek with a gentle hand. And suddenly the thought flashed through her mind that, as yet, he had made no suggestion regarding their wedding day. Did it matter? she thought understandingly. Phillip was the kind of man who did one thing at a time. The engagement came first; the wedding would follow. But, as if sensing her thoughts, Phillip said: 'About a year or so, don't you think, Janet? That will give us time to look around for a house, and I expect you will want to collect a trousseau.'

'A year or so! That seems rather a long time, Phillip.'

'I never believe in rushing things,' he said, but he smiled indulgently, a little pleased with her impatience. 'We can enjoy our engagement meanwhile, you know.'

Which was all right, she thought, for a boy and girl in the throes of first love. But they were not a boy and girl . . .

The thought made her feel guilty. The one which followed made her alarmed. What was it Shaun O'Hara had said about breaking her engagement? Well, a 'year or so' would give him plenty of time . . .

She roused herself. Such thoughts were ridiculous, even dangerous. Besides, Shaun's words meant nothing. He had been flirting with her at that moment—or trying to. Anyone could see that he was not to be taken seriously. There was only one thing Shaun O'Hara could ever be serious about, and that was his work.

CHAPTER THIRTEEN

When a new or unusual operation was to be performed, an air of expectancy seemed to invade the entire hospital.

The day before the operation Andrew McNeil lectured the staff carefully and in detail, impressing upon them their individual responsibilities, and the service he would require from them during that important hour.

'At all costs,' he said, 'we must not fail. It is up to all of us—not myself alone, but each and every one of us—to see that this young man leaves the theatre with every chance of retaining his vision. Alone, I cannot do it. As a team, we can . . .'

Matron visited the patient before his operation. He seemed, as usual, quiet and content. Meg was talking to him as she entered the ward, but stepped aside respectfully. The girl looked strained and tired, Matron observed. Did she, after all, lack the necessary stamina for nursing?

But it was not lack of stamina which caused Meg's fatigue. As the time for Richard's operation had drawn nearer, she had become too keyed up to relax. Janet knew this, although she made no sign. She was following

Matron down the ward now, bringing up the rear behind Sister Marlow. She gave Meg a friendly smile and whispered: 'There's a cup of tea in the kitchen—I should grab it while you can!' Meg gave Janet a grateful glance and departed.

Matron said: 'Well, Dick? And how do you feel this morning?'

Richard smiled at once. He knew her voice well, for she was a frequent visitor at his home.

'Grand, Miss Gamlin.'

'Anything you want?'

'Nothing at all. I'm spoiled to death as it is!'

They laughed together.

'I'm grateful to you and Doctor O'Hara for bringing me to the ward,' he continued. 'I wouldn't be feeling so grand if I were still in solitary confinement.'

'I hope it didn't really seem like that?'

'At times it did.'

'It was your father's wish, you know, and we respected it. And, of course, rest and quietness were essential to you.'

'Rest, perhaps, but the boys in here have helped me more than that deadly quietness. They're a grand lot. The nurses, too.'

Sister Marlow's thin lips unbent slightly. She wanted to say: 'One nurse in particular, I believe?' but her hospital training silenced her.

*　　　*　　　*

In her office, Matron found Andrew McNeil waiting. She was not really surprised. For a long time it had been his habit to visit her before going up to any serious operation. How the custom had started, neither of them really knew. They had, of course, been friends for years. He had come to the hospital as junior house surgeon the year she began her nursing training, and they were the only remaining members of that year's staff. Perhaps this was the root of the bond between them.

Whatever the cause, the bond was strong.

She had his white heather ready, and he smiled as she extended it. No one knew who presented him with that tiny sprig, but it was always there, in the buttonhole of his jacket, when he arrived on the theatre. It remained in the buttonhole, shut away in a metal locker, while he operated. And it was not thrown away until he left the hospital for his well-run bachelor flat.

He glanced down as she placed the heather in position. Strange, the feeling of confidence this tiny gesture gave him. He was feeling nervous, and she knew it. No one else would have suspected, but she, who had known him for so long, was familiar with that betraying symptom—the slight twitching of his left eyebrow which, right from the early days, had given him away. She remembered how, the first time he operated, she had observed it above his white mask; how his eyes had met hers and recognition and acknowledgement had leapt between them. She had been a very unimportant nurse, and he an equally unimportant junior house surgeon. They had traveled a long way together since then, understanding one another, each knowing that the other lived for one thing only—hospital.

She said: 'Good luck, Andrew!'

'Thank you, Hilda.'

For this brief moment, in the sanctity of her office, they shed their formality. He touched her hand gratefully, saying: 'I will be all right, now . . .'

She gave him her gentle smile. He observed, as always, how lovely she was when she smiled. For a brief moment he studied her, realizing for the first time that age had given beauty to this woman. As a girl she had been pleasant, but ordinary. Now prematurely white hair transformed her into a very lovely person—that, and her air of quiet dignity which had been acquired with the years.

She said confidently: 'You are always all right, Andrew, once you start to operate.'

'How well you know me!'

'We know each other well, surely, after all these years?'

He glanced at his watch.

'In five minutes, I must go up. May I spend those five minutes here?'

'Of course.'

She sat down at her desk, pretending to

work.

'I've just been to see young Herrick,' she told him. 'He is amazingly cheerful.'

'I believe O'Hara's idea of giving him companionship was the key to that.'

'Very probably.'

'He will go a long way—O'Hara, I mean.'

'Then let's hope the Royal Rockport doesn't lose him. So often these up-and-coming ones seek fresh fields!'

'Except people like us, Hilda. We plant our roots deep.'

'I like my roots deep. It's a nice feeling. I shall hate digging them up.'

'Digging them up! You will never do that, my dear.'

'I have to retire some day.'

The thought apparently disconcerted him, for he stared in a startled sort of way.

'If it comes to that,' he said bleakly, 'I suppose I shall have to, too . . .'

'Not for years. A man can be a useful surgeon long after a woman has ceased to be a useful nurse.'

'Stop talking like that. You know perfectly well the hospital could never get along without you. *I* couldn't get along without you . . .'

She gave a gentle laugh.

'Eventually, you will both have to. And you will be surprised to find how well you do . . .'

He frowned again as he glanced at his watch.

'I suppose you can't slip up to the theatre?' he asked.

'Unfortunately, no. We have a fresh batch of patients arriving today. I shall be kept busy all morning.'

'It would be nice to think that you were there.'

'With all these students from the London medical schools, there would hardly be room for me!'

'And a lot they will see of this operation, in their screened-off gallery!'

He held out his hand. Lightly, she touched it.

'Good luck,' she said again.

'Thank you, my dear.'

He walked toward the door. Then he turned.

'I almost forgot! Can you drop in for cocktails on Sunday evening? I've Wardour, the plastic man, coming down for the weekend.'

'I should be delighted. How clever of you to get him! He is quite a celebrity,' she teased.

'That is why I invited him!'

Her eyebrows went up in surprise.

'That doesn't sound like you, Andrew.'

He laughed.

'I have an object. A child with a scarred face, who won't accept charity. This is a deep, dark plot to make her.'

She was interested at once.

'Tell me—?'

'A little nurse downstairs—shares a room at the home with Linda Powell.'

'You don't mean Meg Watling! Andrew, how wonderful of you! I've known the child for years and am so very fond of her.'

'It was Linda's idea. She wants her to be examined, and this is the only way we can bring her face to face with someone who can do so. Six-thirty, then, on Sunday?'

'I'll be there,' she told him.

CHAPTER FOURTEEN

There was a light knock upon Matron's door. She called: 'Come in!' and saw, to her surprise, the neat figure of Meg Watling.

'May I speak to you a moment, Matron, please?'

Meg was a little awed by the impressive severity of Matron's office—even by Matron herself. She had expected this moment to be easy, that she would find Miss Gamlin, away from the wards, as friendly and relaxed as in her own home, but this was not the case. She faced a stiff, almost severe figure; an authoritative, forbidding figure seated behind an immense desk—a desk which divided them like the wall of a stronghold. There could be no unbending in such an atmosphere as this, no relaxing of authority.

'What is it, Nurse?'

They might have been strangers. They might never have walked together, in her father's rose gardens, selecting blooms for Hilda Gamlin to take back to hospital. They might never have known each other so well that the secrets of one's heart could be revealed. Had it really been easy to confide in this woman, to tell her of Keith's desertion, to seek her aid in readjusting her life?

Meg's lips moved soundlessly. Matron frowned. Had Meg but known, she was resorting to severity to resist the pity which always moved her when she looked upon this wounded young face. She had to remember that Meg was no different from the rest of the girls here. She was another nurse, and must be treated as such.

'Speak up, child.'

Meg gulped: 'I wish to apply for a transfer to another ward, Matron!'

Miss Gamlin stared. She bit her lower lip to prevent its trembling, for the audacity of a student nurse daring to make such a request to Matron herself was actually funny. Years later, Meg would laugh about it, but right now, Hilda Gamlin realized, the child was in earnest.

'And why, may I ask?'

'It is something quite personal, Matron—'

'There is nothing too personal in this hospital for its Matron to know about.

Everything that goes on here concerns me. Everything, do you understand?'

'Yes, Matron.'

'Then answer my question.'

Silence.

'Do you dislike the ward? Believe me, there are others you would dislike more.'

'It isn't that at all, Matron!'

'Then for the last time, Nurse, I demand an answer!'

'It concerns one of the patients, Matron—'

'Which patient?'

'Richard Herrick.'

'And in what way?'

'I don't want him to see me—ever!'

Matron was quiet. So *that*, she thought, is the root of it . . .

'The other patients see you, Nurse. Why not Herrick?'

'He doesn't know what I look like!'

'The other patients do, my child. Do you find it makes any difference to them?'

Her voice was gentle now, but still firm.

'No, Matron.'

'Then it will make no difference to Richard Herrick. I think you may take my word for that.'

'You mean—you are refusing me a transfer?'

'You will proceed through this hospital as all the nurses do—working upwards, from the bottom, and systematically through all the wards. You will take what comes, child—it is your duty. The supreme lesson a nurse has to learn is obedience. Is that understood?'

Meg's voice was scarcely a whisper: 'Yes, Matron . . .'

'If you find the work distasteful, you know you may resign at the end of three months. Until that time, you will take orders—and carry them out.'

'But I don't wish to resign! I like nursing! But please, *please*, Matron, couldn't you send me to another ward before he is able to see again?'

'But *why*, child?'

'It will be a shock to him!'

'Then why not tell him?' said Matron practically. 'It always helps a patient to realize that others suffer, too.'

'No—I couldn't tell him.'

The young voice had become lifeless, bereft of hope. How could she confess to this austere, aloof figure that she had been foolish enough to allow Richard to believe she was beautiful— worse, that she had allowed him to fall in love with her? How could she disillusion him at this late hour, and what effect would the bitterness of disappointment have upon him?

'I will look for you,' he had said. 'You will be the first person I shall seek—and I will know you, Meg. I will know you!' The proud confidence of his voice, tinged with the tenderness he felt for her, was with her still.

'You realize,' said Matron quietly, 'that he may never see?'

'He is quite certain that he will. He has such faith! Faith like his could not fail him!'

For a moment Matron was quiet. To reveal that her heart was touched by Meg's pitiable fear would, she knew, be a mistake. The girl had chosen a hard way to recover from her suffering, but, in the end, it would be the best way. She had to be made to go forward; not allowed to retreat.

For a brief minute Hilda Gamlin shed her starched authority.

'Meg—look at me.'

The girl lifted her anxious face.

'I told you, when you decided to become a nurse, that you had chosen a hard life— remember? How hard, you are already discovering. And you will continue to discover it, the longer you remain a nurse. But one day you will be glad you chose this profession, and proud. It isn't the glamorous life that posters and films would have us believe—it is something better. It is a completely selfless life, demanding sacrifice and discipline and unending courage. You must display courage now. Go back to your duties—and carry them out.'

The interview was closed. Sick at heart, Meg turned toward the door. As she retreated, her back straightened and her head lifted.

Matron's voice followed her. The starch was

back again.

'One moment, Nurse!'

Meg turned. She stood still, waiting. Her eyes were bright with the pain of unshed tears.

'I presume you left the ward with Sister's permission?'

'Why, no!'

'Do you mean to tell me that you deserted your post?'

'I did not realize—'

'Then the sooner you *do* realize, the better! What you have done is a punishable offense. No one below the rank of Sister can leave the ward without permission, except in the case of emergency. And I believe I saw you running along the corridor this morning. A nurse is only allowed to run on the ward in the case of emergency, also. Otherwise, she conducts herself at all times with decorum. Didn't you learn that at training school?'

'Yes, Matron.'

Miss Gamlin inclined her head in dismissal.

'Then remember in future. You may go.'

But she softened the order with a sudden smile.

'And I should go at the double—as ex-Seaman Gunner Perkins would say.'

A very human chuckle followed Meg from the room.

Descending to Cunningham Ward in the elevator, Meg came face to face with Linda, who looked—as always—cool and poised in her immaculate white coverall. Seeing Meg, her warm smile peeped out.

'Just the girl I wanted to see!' she cried. 'You are off duty on Sunday evening, aren't you? I've accepted an invitation for both of us—cocktails at a friend's.'

'Thank you, Linda.'

'Six-thirty, or thereabouts?'

'I don't come off duty until six on Sunday, but I'll try to be ready in time. I've never been to a cocktail party. Will it be very sophisticated?'

'Gracious, no! Wear that little sapphire blue suit of yours and you'll look lovely. By the way, I'm just going down to Cunningham. Could you save me a journey and give this test meal to Sister?'

'I don't think I dare. I shouldn't have left the ward.'

Linda grinned mischievously. 'I see! Don't worry—I won't betray you!' She asked no questions, but chattered on in her animated fashion all the way down to the ward. Luckily for Meg, the corridor was clear and she was able to slip into the ward kitchen without discovery.

'Oh, there you are, Watling!' Janet exclaimed. 'I was just going to look for you— These specimen jars have to be washed, and don't forget to do the sterilizer, will you?' She took the test meal from Linda and finished: 'This Herrick operation has thrown us all

113

behind today.'

'Has the patient come down yet?'

'Not yet.'

'How soon will they know if it was successful?'

Janet answered: 'Mr. McNeil will know if he manages to seal the retina, or not. If he does, then sight is guaranteed and all the boy has to have is a month's solid rest after it. A brief taste of darkness, to allow the the welding to set, then he can sample a little light, increasing the amount daily.' Janet finished proudly: 'If this operation is a success, Meg, it will be another triumph for the Royal Rockport Hospital!'

'You're proud of this place, aren't you, Janet? I don't know how you are going to tear yourself away from it!'

Janet said briskly: 'Rot! I'll jump at the chance to give up nursing. Don't we all?'

'Not all. Take Sister Marlow—'

Janet answered frankly: 'Much as we admire her, do we want to become like her? At her job she's superb. But the average woman doesn't want to spend her life in hospital.'

'What about Matron?'

'I can't understand why she has never married. She's a lovely woman, Meg, with a heart as gentle as a mother's underneath her starch.'

Continuing on her way, Meg thought: I believed that, too, until today . . .

114

A door swung vigorously upon its hinges as Hunter, a fellow student nurse, burst in.

'He's coming down! They're bringing him back to the ward! He's on his way now . . .'

Meg was frozen into immobility. Then, slowly, she turned.

'Tell me,' she whispered, and could go no further. There was no need, for Hunter continued in excitement: 'They say it was wonderful! I heard Doctor O'Hara discussing it with Doctor Chambers. He said the patient can't fail to see again—imagine that!'

The door swung behind her. Meg could hear the girl's feet speeding along the passage outside, and she thought, in a queer, detached fashion: 'She's running . . . she shouldn't be running . . . not on duty . . .'

But her heart was singing a paean of praise even as, in its innermost corners, it wept in anguish.

For soon—too soon—she would have to face him. He would see her as she really was. He would see the dreadful reality, and turn from it—as Keith had done. And the moment would be more terrible than before.

CHAPTER FIFTEEN

Unexpectedly, that afternoon, Night Sister went down with 'flu, and Janet, who had achieved bows to her cap, but had not yet been elevated to the rank of Sister, found herself temporarily appointed in her place. After tea, therefore, she went off duty to snatch some rest before starting her new duties. All the operational cases in Cunningham were now at the recuperative stage; even the laparotomy seemed hopeful and all Richard Herrick required was careful supervision and rest, until the big moment when, little by little, he would be allowed to see the light of day.

The ward was full and no further operational cases would be admitted until a bed became vacant. Perkins, irrepressibly, cocked a cheerful eyebrow at Janet as she went off duty, and piped: 'So you'll be 'olding me 'and in the middle of the night, eh, Nurse? That's a bit of luck!' She gave him her friendly smile and said: 'If you don't sleep, Gunner, I'll drug you! I know how to deal with patients who cause disturbances in the night!' But as she went on her way she thought: Dear old Perky—how the ward will miss him when he goes! After so many years in residence, he seemed like the heartbeat of Cunningham Ward.

Janet disliked night duty; many nurses did. A ten-hour vigil with depleted staff in the loneliness of shadowed wards could be tedious to the point of exhaustion—and worse than that was the feeling of solitary responsibility.

Doctor O'Hara came down to the ward after the evening rush was over and the patients had been settled for the night. It was a surprise to Janet, who had expected to see the relief. It was equally a surprise to Shaun to find her.

She took her flashlight and went with him along the ward, pausing beside Richard Herrick's bed and observing how profoundly and peacefully he slept. He had remained drugged since the operation and had, therefore, been unaware of Meg's vigilance. At the Royal Rockport a student nurse was usually appointed to remain beside a patient after an operation, with surgical bowl at the ready, but in Richard's case this had been unnecessary. He had taken the shock to his nervous system with characteristic fortitude, even beneath the merciful oblivion of an anaesthetic, but Meg had hovered over him like a guardian angel. Janet's heart had stirred in sympathy.

It was very plain indeed that Meg was in love with him. Sister Marlow's observation had been right. When the child approached Richard's bed her face revealed a tender concern which made Janet's throat ache and her heart stir with envy.

But now Meg had gone off duty and Richard lay asleep. Shaun felt his pulse expertly, giving a professional nod of satisfaction. As they withdrew he said: 'McNeil did a magnificent job. You didn't witness it, I suppose? A pity. I managed to duck duty for half an hour and slipped up to the theatre. Of course I couldn't see the whole performance, but what I saw impressed me. The hospital is fortunate in its senior visiting surgeon.'

Janet agreed. When they were on duty together like this, when they stuck to the subject of work and avoided personalities, she and Doctor O'Hara discovered a surprising kinship. Right from the beginning, when he had intruded into her conversation with Linda, she had felt nothing but animosity toward this man and had firmly believed it impossible to feel anything else. But it was amazing how his appearance in the ward, especially now, when the entire responsibility for these patients rested on her slim shoulders, gave her a feeling of confidence. Dislike him as she did, she had to admit that as a doctor she could not hope to work with anyone better.

He lingered beside the aged seaman, who was slowly pulling around. The man was conscious now and, at this moment, merely lingering upon the borderland of sleep. Even so, with his withered eyelids closed, he sensed Doctor O'Hara's nearness and a corner of his wrinkled old mouth tilted in a welcoming smile.

'Knew you'd come, sir,' he murmured, and Shaun's hand fell sympathetically, comfortingly, upon his.

'Of course,' grinned Shaun. 'In a little while we'll be doing more than exchanging polite good nights, you and I. We'll be splicing the mainbrace together—what d'you say to that?'

The faded eyes, opened now, twinkled in the shadowed light from Janet's flashlight.

'It's a nice idea, sir, but I won't be allowed my ration of rum any more, will I?'

Shaun gave him a conspiratorial grin.

'Well watered down, skipper, and called by some other name, perhaps!' And, with a reassuring nod and smile, he went on his way.

Outside the ward, Janet said: 'Did you mean that?'

The tenderness in Shaun's voice surprised her when he answered: 'Why not? He can't last long in this world, even if he recovers. He's too old, Janet, and he has lived a hard life. So why shouldn't he enjoy his ration of rum if it helps him to believe that he is still an able-bodied seaman?'

And his tone was so kind and gentle that it touched her heart.

She said impulsively: 'My junior is making tea, Doctor—as you probably know, we drink quantities on night duty. When your round is finished, would you like a cup?'

His teasing smile peeped out.

'Well now, and that's kind, to be sure—and not an invitation I'd be refusing, Nurse!'

When he teased her, his brogue was always more pronounced. She turned her head away, annoyed with herself for allowing a tell-tale color to steal to her cheeks. Annoyed, too, because he took this conventional offer as an 'invitation.' How like him! How aggravatingly, tantalizingly like him! Why did he always make her feel that any friendly overture on her part harbored more than friendliness? And what a pity it was that a man she could like so much professionally was so irritating personally!

Leaving the private wards, he said: 'And when is the happy date to be, Nurse?'

She answered stiffly: 'I presume you mean by that the date of my wedding, Doctor. If so, it will be precisely when we are ready.'

'Or when Augustus is?' he taunted. 'If it were me, now, I'd carry you off like the overbearing Irishman I am. There's a little place in Killarney which would make an ideal spot for a honeymoon. Shall I recommend it to Augustus?'

She answered furiously: 'We will decide for ourselves where to spend our honeymoon, Doctor O'Hara.'

He chuckled.

'But can't a patriotic Irishman recommend the beauties of his own country? Have you ever visited Ireland, Janet?'

'Never.'

'Ah, but you should!' he whispered. 'It would enchant you.'

'I am much too practical to be easily enchanted.'

'That you are not, young woman! Underneath that stiff uniform of yours you are a complete sentimentalist, yearning for romance. Oh yes, you are! You've been looking for it all your life and envying those who found it. You're even trying to find it with Augustus—God knows why! There must be plenty of other men in your life. Or could be.'

'Nurses don't have much opportunity to meet men, Doctor—not nearly so much as people imagine. Patients are rarely "romantic," as you put it, and very soon forget a nurse once they are cured.'

'But what about the medical staff? Oh, I know all the unwritten laws of hospital life, but nurses and doctors *do* meet, you know.' He grinned at her mockingly. 'Take us, for instance. We bump into one another quite a bit, don't we?'

She retorted scathingly: 'Doctors! Heaven forbid!'

'And what's wrong with doctors, pray?'

'Everything! They're conceited, opinionated, and quite incapable of discussing anything but "shop" when they go out with a girl. Imagine having medicine for breakfast, lunch and dinner!'

'You should try me,' he said complacently. 'My range of conversation would astonish you!' He held open the kitchen door for her to pass through, but before she did so he added: 'Tell me truthfully—do you really fancy hospital accounts and agendas as a diet? I am quite sure dear Augustus will even talk about them in his sleep!'

She ignored that. She crossed to the enamel table where the junior nurse had left the tea. With a second year nurse the girl sat at the end of the kitchen, cutting slices of bread for breakfast. A patient's bell rang imperatively and the second year nurse went to answer it. Janet poured the tea and drank it appreciatively, wishing that Shaun O'Hara would drink his, and go. But he seemed in no hurry. He straddled a chair and grinned at the younger girl.

'I always wonder,' he said, 'why some hospitals don't install bread-slicing machines. Or would it cheat the night nurses of their occupation?'

'We have a bread-cutter, sir,' said the junior, 'but it has gone wrong.'

'Let me have a look at it! I love meddling with things mechanical—'

Janet interposed swiftly: 'I shouldn't if I were you, Doctor. A man is coming to fix it tomorrow—'

'And I might make it worse?' he laughed. 'What difference will that make, if it is out of order already?'

He was quite determined; it was useless even to try to get rid of him. Janet took out her note book and began to record, in her neat, firm writing, the patients' individual doses and times of administration. She heard Shaun fiddling with the bread-cutter, while the junior stood by, watching and admiring. Janet said briskly: 'If you have nothing to do just now, Nurse, please go down to the dispensary for the oxygen cylinder.'

The girl looked at her in surprise.

'Are we going to need it tonight, Sister?'

'No—but its place is here, not down in the dispensary. It was sent down for replenishing. Run along.'

The girl departed. Shaun, head bent, said quietly: 'Angry with me, Janet?'

'Of course not.'

He gave a mock shiver.

'The ice in Sister Marlow's voice, my dear, has already begun to tinge your own. Are you aware of that?'

She was horrified at the idea. Shaun came toward her and, leaning across the table, looked her squarely in the face.

'It is true, whether you like it or not. Hospitals do things to women, Janet—things I don't like. And I'd like them even less in you. Excessive efficiency chills a man—except a man like myself, too hot-blooded to be easily chilled. Or a man like Augustus, so pedantic that he even admires officiousness in a woman.' He held up a swift, restraining hand. 'Don't interrupt!' he warned. 'Nothing will stop me now, so don't even try. I've been wanting to say this ever since I met you.'

He seized her squarely by the shoulders, forced her to her feet and compelled her toward the small, square mirror which the nurses had hung upon the wall. 'Look at yourself, Janet! What are you doing to that face of yours? Look at your mouth—it wasn't meant to be firm and controlled like that—it was meant for tenderness and laughter! For this—'

And he spun her round, almost savagely, imprinting a strong, dominating kiss upon her lips, pinioning her with his powerful arms so that she could not thrust him away. And when it was over he laughed, with his lips against her hair, knocking her starched cap awry and twisting her immaculately tied bows beneath her chin.

'Darling!' he whispered. 'You were meant to be loved, to be a woman—not a piece of starch! You were meant to be a man's wife, not his slave or admiring shadow! That is what Augustus will do to you, that is what he wants of you. You'll be exchanging the discipline of a hospital for the solitary discipline of serving one man for the rest of your life! Think of it!'

She pushed him violently on one side. She was sobbing with anger.

'How dare you! How *dare* you!' she panted, straightening her cap and bows with agitated fingers.

'Is that all you can say?' he mocked. 'How *dare* you, Shaun! Yes, that's my name and one day you will be using it—and not in that tone of voice, either. You'll be saying it with love, even with passion . . .'

'Rubbish! You just don't know me, Doctor O'Hara! I have no time for sentiment. I'm not capable of passion. I want peace and a quiet happiness and, believe me, I'm going to find them—with Phillip.'

At that, he laughed even more.

'It's yourself you're not knowing, Janet. You've clamped down on sentiment, smothered it, shunned it. It's afraid you are— afraid of letting your natural instincts conquer you. And what will be happening? Either you'll be staying forever in this hospital, becoming more and more like Sister Marlow, or you'll become Augustus' idea of the ideal woman— drab, respectable, and a prig. Either thought fair breaks my heart!'

'Turn off that Irish brogue,' she cried, 'and go away! I won't listen to you!'

'But you *will* listen!' he commanded, his voice sinking to such a passionate note of determination that her anger quelled before it. And suddenly she was quiet and passive, ridden by a fear she had never felt before. The fear that what he said was true . . .

She felt his arms go about her again and his lips come down on hers—gently this time, but warm with passion.

'Does he ever kiss you like that?' he whispered. 'Does he ever make that lovely flush come to your face? Does he make those eyes betray you? And now you are trembling—that is desire, my love, the desire you have kept so firmly suppressed all these years—'

She pressed the back of her hand against her mouth and bit her knuckles to stifle an unbidden sob. And Shaun said with infinite tenderness: 'Now I've made you cry—and I didn't want to do that. But thank God you can, Janet!'

'Go—please go! Someone will come—'

He went to the other side of the room and stood looking at her, smiling his tender, disturbing smile.

'Some day, Janet, I am going to make a real woman out of you, as an Irishman I know did to the woman he loved. She came of a snobbish, wealthy household and was as repressed as the whole of her stiff-necked family. He carried her off, the day before her marriage to a horse-riding, hard-drinking, well-bred bore. The Irishman hadn't any money, but he gave that woman more riches than she had ever possessed in her life—he gave her love and happiness and a lot of laughter. Three kids, too, to bring up in a wild Irish dell. There was never any money and they all had to work. That,' he finished, 'was why I qualified so late in life. I had to work hard to earn enough for my medical training.'

She looked at him in inquiry and he nodded his attractive head.

'Yes, the Irishman was my father. They gave us a wonderful life, those two, because they didn't deny love and weren't afraid of passion. They took life by the shoulders and shook everything out of her that she had to give. And enjoyed it all! We'll do the same, Janet m' darling. Don't you realize *I* am the man for you?'

She took a deep breath.

'Shaun O'Hara, are you by any chance asking me to marry you?'

He laughed heartily at that.

'Not on your life, my girl! I'm *telling* you you're going to. Just as soon as I've broken this ridiculous engagement of yours. I did tell you I intended to, didn't I?'

CHAPTER SIXTEEN

Andrew McNeil lived in a spacious, well-appointed flat just outside Rockport. It was at the top of a converted wing in what had once been a country mansion. The house still retained the elegance of former centuries, despite the building contractor's ingenuity, and

Andrew's home reflected his appreciation of all things beautiful.

It had a dignity and graciousness which was, somehow, characteristic of the man himself, but it also had a warm, human touch which put visitors immediately at their ease.

Brett Rogers, entering the wide hall, felt his innate shyness begin to evaporate. He had been reluctant to come and, as he drove from his own little flat overlooking the harbor, had wondered quite frankly why he had accepted McNeil's unexpected invitation. Apart from professional contact within the hospital, they never met, and although their mutual liking for one another was a very sincere thing, Brett had never expected McNeil's friendship to extend beyond the sphere of their work. People who spent their lives within hospital walls rarely wanted to meet again outside them.

Perhaps, he thought, as he drove his powerful, low-slung car up the steep hill from the town, he had come simply because Sunday was always a long and lonely day. Perhaps he had accepted because social invitations so rarely came his way. Perhaps curiosity alone had brought him. Whatever the reason, here he was, parking his car in the impressive drive, climbing the wide marble staircase which led to McNeil's apartment, walking into the long, high-ceilinged drawing-room which seemed, at this moment, to house a surprising number of guests. The surge of their conversation came to Brett like the hum of an advancing tide.

McNeil's welcoming hand was extended and his friendly arm propelled Brett farther into the room. He found a tray at his elbow and Matron's charming face smiling at him through the welter of unfamiliar ones. His eyes searched the room, and he knew then when disappointment stabbed him, why he had really come. He had hoped to meet Linda here. Because it was McNeil's party, he had expected Linda to be here . . .

The sea of faces stretched before him like a field of animated mushrooms—none, in the suffocating fog of his shyness, had any great meaning for him. Once Andrew McNeil moved on to attend to other guests, Brett found himself floundering, as usual, in the deep tide of his self-consciousness. Lacking social small talk, he sought some corner in which to hide, and, seeing a wide window-seat flanking a deep bay, he edged toward it. It looked secluded and deserted, just the place for a man who could not fit into a smart, sophisticated gathering.

But when he reached the window-seat Brett found it occupied. A shabby, unobtrusive little man sat there—bald and tubby and elderly. Like a plump gnome without beard or cap. His eyes were like bright berries and his skin was wrinkled. He nodded his head cheerfully at Brett and said: 'Come and hide with me . . .'

and smiled in a conspiratorial way. It was as if he recognized Brett's shyness and understood it.

The man wasn't shy himself—just impatient of social chatter and party manners. Somehow Brett knew that without being told. 'At least the drinks are good,' the old man said, 'if you like fancy drinks, but I wouldn't be here if my wife hadn't dragged me.'

Brett smiled, wondering who, out of this medley of well-dressed women, could possibly be married to this shabby, friendly little man.

Brett settled himself upon the window-seat. 'Have a sandwich,' said the gnome, thrusting a plate at him. 'Take half a dozen—they're so small you can eat 'em at a swallow. Why do people serve things like these instead of the good old-fashioned kind which really satisfied a man?'

Brett smiled again. The man's frankness appealed to him.

'What are you doing here?' the voice went on. A surprisingly cultured one. But how badly he was dressed! Shabby old tweed jacket; flannel trousers sagging at the knees. He might have been the gardener, wandered in by mistake. Out of the pocket of his jacket protruded a rolled-up cap. Shabby, also. Seeing Brett's glance, its owner chuckled.

'Had to do something with it!' he said. 'Couldn't hand a cap like that to McNeil's stiff-necked butler! Shoved it out of sight before my

130

wife rang the bell. Didn't want to embarrass her. Have another sandwich—or one of those sausage things on sticks. If they were twice as big, on the end of a fork, they'd be worth eating.'

Brett laughed and helped himself. 'Nice view from here,' he commented, glancing out of the window. Below spread impressive grounds, and beyond lay the sea, swirling like a foaming garland on the edge of the shore. Not far away he could see Heath Hill, Linda's home. It stood out, rather splendid and imposing, against a background of oak and beech.

The old man said: 'Yes, a good view. This is a good part of the world, my boy. You a native of Rockport?'

'No. London. Highgate, to be exact.'

'Working at the hospital?'

'Pathology.'

The stranger regarded him with interest.

'Then you're Rogers! I've heard of you, of course.'

'Why "of course"? I'm only one member of the hospital staff.'

'You underrate yourself.' The bright, berry-like eyes regarded him shrewdly. 'You're chief pathologist, aren't you? That's a position to be respected.' The old man looked right through him, summing him up, seeing so much that Brett would have kept hidden.

'It isn't respect I want,' Brett muttered

defensively.

'Then what do you want?'

'Just my work.'

'Nonsense. You want what every young man wants—friendship, and more besides. Married?' he barked abruptly.

'Of course not.'

'Why "of course not"? It would be more natural if you were.'

Brett was silent. Married, he thought. Me? Never. Who would marry a moody, inarticulate boor such as I? He didn't utter the thought, but the shabby man sensed it.

'Have another drink, Doctor—' He thrust a glass before Brett, continuing amiably: 'The only thing to do at these affairs is take what comes round on the trays, until you can make a convenient get-away. Where are you going when you make your escape?'

'Back to my flat,' Brett told him. Where else was there to go in Rockport on a Sunday night? He had a comfortable armchair and some books awaiting him.

'Any beer there?'

Brett gave his sudden, spontaneous smile.

'Plenty!'

'Then I'll come with you. May I? These fancy cocktails aren't really in my line. But my wife, bless her, won't want to leave for ages yet. She won't miss me if I go. So long as I put in an appearance, she doesn't mind if I leave early. An understanding soul, beneath her anxiety to observe the social conventions. Funny creatures, women; set such value by surface things.' He finished abruptly: 'Why d'you keep looking at that house over there?'

'Heath Hill? Just admiring it.'

'Many people do, I believe.'

He gave Brett the impression that splendor in any form did not appeal to him. Whoever he was, whatever he was, he had an innate simplicity which appealed to Brett. He felt his heart warming to the friendly gnome—or perhaps it was the cocktails. Whatever the cause, Brett found himself talking easily and unself-consciously. Of medicine, of research, of the hospital. The old man was a good listener, only prompting with an occasional comment or question. He was, it was plain, deeply interested in Brett's work. Alone in their isolated corner, they forgot the rest of the party. And Andrew McNeil, busy exchanging social courtesies with his guests, observed their seclusion and envied it. He was wondering why he had ever hit upon this idea of entertaining on a Sunday evening, and was about to say as much to Hilda Gamlin when he observed that she was deep in conversation with the guest of the evening—Simon Wardour. Indeed, so interested did she appear that she hadn't a glance to spare for Andrew. He felt a sudden twinge of envy, of annoyance, of thwarted anger.

Wardour was an interesting man, of course,

and had proved an entertaining week-end guest, but Andrew had hardly expected him to monopolize Hilda all the evening . . .

He wished Linda would hurry and bring her little friend. After all, that was the object of this evening's party, his reason for inviting Wardour. He had told the man all about Meg's injury and the hopes they entertained for her recovery. Wardour had been more than interested. Andrew glanced at his watch impatiently, and saw to his surprise that it was only seven. The little nurse didn't come off duty, Linda had told him, until six, after which she had to change. They would take a taxi, Linda had promised, and come as quickly as they could—which meant that they should be here at any moment now. And after that, thought Andrew with bachelor selfishness, perhaps I will be allowed to have my friends to myself! Which meant, of course, Hilda Gamlin. All the rest were mere social acquaintances, duty invitations.

Seeing Andrew's frown, the old man on the window-seat chuckled. Brett's glance questioned him.

'McNeil,' the gnome explained. 'He is experiencing what he should have experienced long ago. Jealousy.'

'Jealousy! Of what? Of whom?'

'Of his guest star. He's got Wardour, the plastic surgeon, here tonight. Didn't you know?'

Brett didn't. This had been an unexpected invitation and he knew none of the other guests.

The old man continued: 'Don't know what he has invited him for. Never known McNeil to lionize anyone. There must be something behind it.'

'But why the jealousy? Surely their spheres don't overlap professionally?'

'Lord, no! It's Matron. Wardour has talked to her, and no one else, ever since she arrived. And McNeil doesn't like it . . .'

'But why should he object?'

'You're very obtuse, young man. Because they've been friends for years. And why the devil they haven't married beats me. Too absorbed in that hospital, is *my* guess.'

Brett stared. Matron? Married to Andrew McNeil? Impossible. Ridiculous. Their names were never even linked. Whoever this shabby little man was, he was very ignorant of things which were common knowledge at the hospital.

He gave a short laugh.

'You're barking up the wrong tree,' he told the gnome. 'Matron and McNeil might be friends, but it is common knowledge whom he intends to marry.'

The bright eyes regarded him questioningly.

'And who has Common Knowledge chosen?'

'His predecessor's daughter—Linda Powell.'

The gnome rocked with laughter.

'It is true,' Brett assured him. 'I've heard them talking together—on the phone. She is my assistant. And, if you ask me, there is a lot to be said for such an alliance.'

'An alliance between youth and age? Do you really think there is anything to be said in favor of it?'

'It would be an alliance between one of a certain social standing and another of equal social standing.' Brett was unaware of the wistfulness in his voice. 'Her parents are all for it, I gather.'

'That's very interesting.'

'Of course, he's a friend of the family; a surgeon as distinguished as her father; same background and all that. Besides, I imagine Mrs. Powell wants a successful marriage for her daughter.'

'Show me a mother who doesn't! Isn't that only natural?'

'Quite natural, I suppose.'

'And what of the girl's father? Since you know so much about it, young man, answer me that.'

'Oh, he's sure to be set on it, too. Discovered McNeil. Made him.'

'So he'd like to keep him in the family?'

'Why not?' Brett's glance travelled through the window again and he nodded toward the distant house. 'Look at Heath Hill—a girl who came from a home like that would be expected to make a distinguished marriage.'

The old man finished his drink and put down his glass.

'Clever of you to have worked it out so neatly, Doctor.'

Brett made no answer. He finished his own drink moodily. It was all very well, thought he, for an old man like this to pass judgment, but what did he know of the strong social standards observed in Rockport?

'Ever meet her father?' the old man piped.

'Never. Don't have to. I can imagine what he is like.'

'The male counterpart of her mother, eh?'

'Why not? Like takes to like.'

The old man gave a mock shudder. 'Clichés,' he murmured. 'Wouldn't have expected a man like you to use them.' He regarded Brett with a certain pitying amusement which, fortunately, Brett did not see, for at that moment he was staring across the room. Linda was just arriving, with that little nurse from Cunningham Ward. Linda's advent was like a ray of sunshine penetrating a darkened room. Brett's heart gave a sudden quiver, then was still.

The old man followed his glance. He smiled. He said nothing, but watched and waited as Linda made her halting progress across the room. First, she met Andrew, who advanced to her with hands extended— relieved because she had come. Brett, of course, saw only his eager greeting, the encircling arm which fell across her shoulders, drawing her through the little crowd to the distant corner where Hilda Gamlin and the famous plastic surgeon sat together. Andrew's hospitable welcome included the shy student nurse, and into her nervous hand he put a glass of sherry. He was looking down at her with a kindly, reassuring smile, for it was plain that Meg was most painfully ill at ease—overcome by the sophistication about her, by the unexpectedness of finding herself entertained socially in the home of so great a man.

Meg looked up at Andrew McNeil and smiled her thanks. Away from the hospital he was even more human than he had been in the ward. At the last minute she had shirked this party, had begged Linda to excuse her, but Linda had been adamant. 'You can't back out now!' she cried. 'I've accepted for both of us!' And Meg had no choice but to come.

And then Andrew was introducing Simon Wardour to Meg, murmuring their names as casually and correctly as if it were just an ordinary introduction. The man smiled at her and said: 'I see you have a drink—what about one of these canapés to go with it?' And somehow Meg found herself seated alone with him, chatting quite easily, while Matron disappeared with Mr. McNeil.

Linda turned away—then stood still, staring across the room at the big bay window where

138

Brett Rogers sat with a shabby, elderly little man. For one brief moment she stood there, then began to wend her way toward them. And Meg was left alone with her companion.

She turned to him, smiling at something he had said, glad she had found someone so ordinary to talk to. It was quite obvious that he could not possibly be anyone important.

CHAPTER SEVENTEEN

Linda was waylaid by her mother's scented bosom, which protruded—bejewelled—across her path. They kissed. They smiled. They were very fond of one another, even though they had so little in common.

'Dear child,' Elizabeth Powell murmured, 'thank goodness you have abandoned that depressing nurses' home for one evening . . .'

Linda laughed.

'Darling, it isn't nearly so bad as you think. In fact, I love it. I enjoy myself there . . .' She glanced over her shoulder at the bay window, and Brett, seeing her smile and the friendly little nod his companion sent in response, said in surprise: 'I didn't realize you knew Miss Powell . . .'

The old man murmured: 'As well as a man of my age might be expected to know a young girl.' And he held out his hands in greeting as

Linda joined them. She stooped and planted an affectionate kiss upon his cheek and exclaimed: 'Father, how lovely! I didn't expect to find you here . . .'

She broke off, looking at Brett. There was a horrified consternation in his eyes which she could not understand. He rose to his feet, stammering incoherently in answer to her polite greeting. She said: 'I'm glad you two have got together—introductions are so tiresome and I always seem to get them round the wrong way!'

Her father answered easily: 'Doctor Rogers and I have been having a most interesting conversation—and he has promised to share some beer with me at his flat'—his kindly old eyes surveyed the younger man and he promptly finished—'one of these evenings.'

Brett swallowed. May the heavens cover me and the earth bury me! he thought wretchedly. May the gods curse me for a blundering fool! I've got to get out of here! I've got to get away . . .

But he carried the moment off with surprising sang-froid.

'Any evening you care to drop in, sir,' he said politely. 'Number three, Harbor Court. About seven—'

And, murmuring a quiet good-night, he crossed to his host, thanked him for a pleasant evening, and departed.

*   *   *

Linda sat down beside her father.

'So you've met him, Daddy . . .'

'And like him,' he finished.

Her hand clutched his arm eagerly. He felt it tremble.

'Really, darling?'

'Really, my dear.'

'He doesn't mean to be rude, you know. Going off like that—abruptly—'

'Merely the action of a shy young man who feels he has made a fool of himself,' said her father gently.

'Why? Had anything gone wrong?'

'Nothing at all, my dear. Nothing at all. But a man always feels a fool when he realizes that he has exposed his heart—to the wrong person.'

Linda looked at him curiously. She was about to ask what he meant when she saw her aunt's bulky figure bearing down upon them. Joseph Powell suppressed a groan.

'Bear up, Daddy,' Linda whispered. 'She can't slap you on the back—it's turned to the window!'

He chuckled.

'One of these days,' he whispered back, 'I shall clap Ethel on the back and see how *she* likes it!'

His sister's voice boomed out: 'So there you are, Linda m' girl! Unbending tonight?'

141

'Unbending, Aunt Ethel?'

'Enough to make yourself sociable, eh? Not often we have the pleasure of meeting you at parties, I must say, but, of course, for *Andrew* it is different!'

And she raised her eyebrows archly. Her monocle fell with a plop onto her well-tailored chest.

'Why "for Andrew?"' Linda echoed coldly.

But Aunt Ethel's volubility could never be chilled. She wagged a thick forefinger at her niece and, sinking her voice to a stage whisper, hissed: 'Better watch out, my girl, or he will slip through your fingers! Look at him, over there with Miss Gamlin . . . And I saw them dining together the other evening—oh, they didn't see me, of course, but I had an unobstructed view of *them*!'

'Of course,' murmured her brother.

'The most secluded table at the Havana! Not often I go there, but quite by chance I went last Friday. Which, I gleaned from the wine waiter, is *their* night!'

'Good sleuthing,' said Linda amiably, 'but you really didn't have to bribe the wine waiter, Aunt Ethel. I could have told you that myself.'

And, with her friendly smile, Linda drifted away. Daddy can take care of Ethel, she thought fondly. There was no one better equipped. Meanwhile, she wanted to be in on this conversation between Meg Watling and the great Wardour. It seemed to be

142

progressing very seriously and—Linda hoped—satisfactorily. She hovered near them until Meg looked up and saw her. And the expression upon Meg's face caused a surge of excitement to stir in Linda's heart, for not since they met had she seen such hope in the child's eyes.

'Linda! Linda—come here!'

Linda went. Her eyes were guileless and questioning. 'Something nice happened, Meg?' she asked lightly, and the child looked up at her, starry-eyed and breathless.

'Something wonderful!'

The great Simon Wardour smiled with admirably assumed gratitude.

'Miss Watling has agreed to do me a favor,' he said. 'She is going to act as human guinea pig for me to practice upon.'

Meg nodded eagerly.

'Mr. Wardour is studying plastic surgery and he is going to experiment upon me!'

Simon Wardour made a negative gesture.

' "Experiment" is hardly the word. I know I can overcome that scar of yours because it is comparatively new and should be easily cured, but it is true that I shall be glad of the opportunity to go to work upon it and I am grateful to Miss Watling for agreeing to let me.' And his bright, observant eyes turned innocently to Linda and, above Meg's excited head, he solemnly winked.

'Wonderful!' cried Linda. 'When does the

treatment start?'

'At once, I hope,' said the surgeon.

Meg's face fell.

'I hadn't thought about that! How silly of me! I won't be able to come to you until my leave—which isn't due for several weeks. I have only just started nursing, you see—'

'You could ask Matron for leave of absence,' suggested Linda.

But Meg, remembering her last interview with Matron, shook her head. She was a nurse now, and with a nurse duty came first, no matter how painful it might be.

She swallowed her disappointment. For one brief, exquisite moment she had thought: Now Richard need never know! Never, never, *never* . . . But that was ridiculous, of course. She could not possibly be cured by the time he was able to see again. Her treatment, Simon Wardour told her, would take some time. She would have to go to his private 'experimental' surgery, perhaps for weeks. It all depended upon how quickly her skin and muscles responded to treatment. There would be a certain amount of plastic surgery needed, combined with skin graft, and results could not be achieved in a matter of days.

Meanwhile, she would have to face Richard. Even now, she could not spare him that shock. A tight, unbearable pain ached in her throat. That she should have this chance, after all these unhappy months, and that it should come so late! That the gods of fortune should suddenly smile upon her and hold out hope undreamed of—and that they should choose so tardy an hour!

It was that first moment which was so important—the moment when he opened his eyes and looked upon her and realized that she had allowed him to cherish a dream . . .

Linda was saying: 'Let's ask Matron now—here she comes.' Meg looked up and saw Hilda Gamlin approaching with Andrew McNeil.

And Linda thought: What a nice-looking couple they make! I do believe love can be as attractive in middle-age as in youth . . .

CHAPTER EIGHTEEN

'But when Matron said "No," Meg looked as if she had been struck, Janet! I couldn't think why. After all, the fact that Simon Wardour *is* going to help her just as soon as Matron can grant her leave is surely the most important fact? And he put the whole idea to her so tactfully, bless him—thanks to Andrew's priming beforehand, I imagine. There he was, the most successful plastic surgeon in England, asking Meg to act as human guinea pig for him! As if she were granting him a favor! I wanted to laugh and cry at the same time. And, of course, Matron was as pleased as any of us—you could see that. "As soon as I can arrange it, Meg," she said, "I promise you shall have prolonged leave until Mr. Wardour is satisfied with the results . . ." Well, really, Janet, what could be more satisfactory than that?'

'Having the treatment right away, of course. Being granted leave immediately. Not entering Cunningham Ward again until she could look the world in the face and not feel afraid of it doing the same to her. Not, of course, that he would still be in Cunningham by that time, but they would meet outside the hospital—I am sure of that.'

Linda looked at Janet in bewilderment.

'Who wouldn't be in Cunningham by that time? Who would she meet outside the hospital?'

'Richard Herrick, of course. Didn't you know they were in love?'

Linda sat down weakly upon her bed.

'Of course,' said Janet, 'you couldn't know, not being in the ward, but everyone else does.'

'Everyone?'

'Sister Marlow, the nurses, the patients— we've all been watching. At first, I didn't notice it particularly. I thought it was just one of those attractions which sometimes spring up between patients and nurses, but I soon realized it was more than that. I even tried to warn the child against a broken heart—think of that! The damage had been done by that time and, funnily enough, the person who saw it first was Sister herself. I always thought she had a stone for a heart. I was wrong.'

'Doesn't he know about Meg's injury?'

'I imagine not. I imagine that's why she is in such a state of anxiety, poor scrap. How was she to know that he would ever see again? How was she to know that she was going to get all tied up emotionally with him?' Janet's face took on an unexpected tenderness. Linda regarded her in surprise. Practical, unsentimental, wholesome Janet—that was how she had always thought of her. This new tenderness, this soft-hearted side, was an unexpected, and very welcome, revelation. What had caused it? What had brought it about? If this was the result of her unromantic engagement to the hospital secretary, then maybe it was a love match, after all . . .

Linda spread herself out, flat upon her back, and stared reflectively at the ceiling. Watching the spiral of smoke trail up from Janet's cigarette, she murmured: 'Poor little Meg—poor, helpless little mite! How can we protect her, Janet?'

'We can't. She's got to go on duty whether she likes it or not. She's got to face him—and he has got to face her. I have a feeling that is more important to her—his seeing her, I mean—than anything else. If he turns from her, Linda, I think the poor child will die—or something inside her will.'

'That wretched Keith Saunders turned from her—I don't suppose she can forget that. I saw him with Shirley Travers at the Royal the other day. They are well matched, those two—selfish through and through, the pair of them. She tried to pump me about Richard Herrick. Seemed mighty anxious to know how he was. I wouldn't put it past her to ditch Keith as heartlessly as he ditched Meg, if it suited her. In other words, if she could still get Richard. She has been trying for years.'

Janet gave a short laugh.

'So I understand. She has called several times to see him, but he has refused all visitors except his parents, so far. I wonder if he will refuse to see her after tomorrow . . .'

'Does the shield come off tomorrow?'

'Briefly. But more and more as the days go by, until it is discarded altogether.'

'Then it is possible he will see Meg tomorrow?'

Janet nodded.

'I suppose,' said Linda almost hopefully, 'there isn't any chance of his failing to see, despite the experts' optimism?'

'None. They tested him today, I understand. Took him into a darkened room and shone a light on to the ceiling above. He saw it—like a white cloud, he said. Your Andrew McNeil was nearly beside himself with joy.'

'Why "my" Andrew McNeil?'

'Isn't he?'

'Certainly not! Don't tell me *you* credit this ridiculous association I am supposed to be involved in?'

'Sorry, Linda. I did wonder, I admit.'

'Then cease to.' Linda's attractive mouth twisted in a secret smile. She had a wide, generous mouth which parted on even white teeth. Janet regarded her with envy. I wish I had her looks! she thought. I wish my hair was that lovely, rich brunette and my eyelashes as long as those!

Janet sighed. She had slipped along for a quiet cigarette and a chat before going on night duty.

She crushed out her cigarette, crossed to Linda's mirror and straightened her cap. Linda watched her as she donned her mask of efficiency and realized with sharp, pleasurable surprise that her friend's air of efficiency *was* but a mask.

'Janet,' she said unexpectedly, 'you've blossomed!'

Janet swung round and stared at her.

'What do you mean?'

Linda sat up. Her long slender legs dangled over the side of the bed.

'Just what I say. Something has happened to you, Janet. What is it? What caused it?'

'You're talking nonsense!' Janet turned back to the mirror and began to straighten the bows beneath her chin, but her fingers betrayed her. They trembled, which was

149

annoying. She hid them beneath her starched apron.

'Know something, Janet Humphrey? I think you are in love . . .'

'Of course I am.'

'But you didn't look like this when you became engaged to Augustus—'

'Phillip,' Janet murmured automatically.

'He'll always be Augustus to me. And to others.'

'Others?' demanded Janet sharply. Linda looked at her for a long moment.

Footsteps sounded in the courtyard outside. Janet glanced out, glad of an excuse to avert her tell-tale face.

'Day nurses coming off,' she said. 'I'd better go down—'

'You don't have to be on duty until your staff have taken over—stay another minute. We get no chance to talk when you're on nights.'

'I know, but I like to do an early round.'

'You can't do that until the nurses have settled all the patients. You are too conscientious sometimes, Jan.'

'So is someone else, apparently.' Janet's glance travelled across the courtyard to the main hospital building. Right at the top, in a window which was normally darkened by now, shone a beam of fluorescent light. 'That moody doctor you work for is still hard at it!'

Linda hurried to the window, saying

indignantly: 'He isn't moody! He's shy, that's all. He has an outsize inferiority complex—heaven knows why! Brainy people often have . . .'

Janet turned and looked at her, aware of surprise because Linda defended Brett Rogers so vigorously. She always stuck up for him, of course, but this anger was based upon something deeper than loyalty. She saw a vexed frown pucker Linda's brow.

'It must be Brett,' she murmured; 'it can't be anyone else . . .' She gave a little sigh of impatience—the kind a mother gives over a stubborn child. 'How like him! I expect he's working on that serum for Doctor Chambers—what a plague that man is! Came up to the lab. raising dust this afternoon because we hadn't sent it down by noon—didn't seem to realize that we've been rushed off our feet all day. It has been one of *those* days,' she finished, staring at the laboratory window anxiously.

'And now it seems your dear pathologist is turning it into one of those nights,' finished Janet lightly. 'Why should you worry?'

Linda made no answer. She turned her back upon the lab. window. She tried to turn her back upon the picture of Brett still stooping over his work bench, those tired little shadows which came beneath his eyes when he overworked growing deeper as the night wore on. As Janet said, why should she worry? But she did.

He would forget to eat, she knew. He would work on, up there in the silent laboratory, forgetful of time. Forgetful of himself. Forgetful of the world, no doubt. She knew that work could give a man satisfaction, but Brett needed other things as well. Things material and spiritual. Food, care—and a woman's love.

'Here comes Meg,' said Janet, still at the window. 'She looks all in—pale as a little ghost.'

'Oh, Janet, what *can* we do for her?'

'No more than is already being done. After all, this chance to be treated by Simon Wardour is more than we could have hoped for a short while ago.'

'Yes, I know. But if only I had realized the need for haste!'

'If only Matron realized it!' echoed Janet.

CHAPTER NINETEEN

'Good evening, Janet—or should I call you Sister now?' said Shaun O'Hara.

'You should,' Janet agreed calmly.

'I have come to assist you on your ward round.'

'Thank you, Doctor.'

'Or to let you assist on mine . . .'

'Thank you, Doctor.'

Shaun suppressed a chuckle. Janet had put on all her starch tonight. He waved a friendly hand toward Linda Powell, who suddenly appeared, clad in her white coverall, and went up in the elevator toward the laboratory. They were certainly keen on their work, the pathologist and his assistant. Shaun turned to make the comment to Janet, but she was looking stiffly ahead and had not seen her friend, and the sudden realization that Janet had the most tantalizing and illogical sort of nose made him forget Linda Powell. He laughed outright and said: 'Ever study it in a mirror?'

She turned to him and said coolly: 'I have no idea, Doctor, of what you are talking.'

'Your nose,' he answered imperturbably. 'It is the most misdesigned nose I have ever seen. Completely unconventional—perhaps that is why I like it. Conventionality and respectability are such boring qualities, don't you agree? But to get back to your nose, Janet—it is characteristic of you.'

'In what way?' she asked unwillingly. Since the night he had kissed her and done such disturbing things to her heart she had resolved to be very frigid indeed with Doctor O'Hara, but when she actually came into contact with him, nothing proved more difficult. He had a disarming way of shattering her defenses— lightly, casually, as if a flick of the finger. What could a girl do with a man who positively refused to be snubbed? How could she withstand a smile so irresistible, a brogue so attractive, and conversation so provocative? Even though, when away from him, Janet could think of all the things she would say when next they met—aloof, frigid, chilling remarks which would soon put him in his place—these, somehow, never had the chance to be uttered for the simple reason that Shaun's conversation was so unpredictable. As now.

'It starts,' he said earnestly as they walked down the corridor to Cunningham, 'as if it intended to be a straight and classical nose, then it hovers on the borders of conventionality—a nose just like any other nose—and then, provocatively, it changes its mind. It thwarts convention and becomes quite definitely individual, almost impertinent, tilting upwards with an air of insouciance and gay bravado!'

Against her will, Janet laughed. Somehow, he always made her laugh, this mad Irishman. She was unaware that when she laughed her pleasant, ordinary face—her face which could be, as Shaun had warned her, almost chilling— lit up with a transforming radiance. Shaun looked down at her (she came barely up to his shoulder, for he was a tall man) and thought: When we are married, she will laugh all the time. I will make her . . .

He said solemnly: 'Oh, I like your nose,

154

Nurse, please believe that! I am not deriding it. My analysis is intended to convey my approval—nothing else. I am only wondering which characteristic is going to win—the respectability, or the bravado. The conventional instinct, or the impertinent one. I hope the latter. A girl with a nose like that should have thrown her cap over the windmill long ago—but I suppose that *would* have spoiled its starch!'

She turned away to hide her smile. She absolutely refused to give this man the satisfaction of seeing her response. She mustered self-control and said with magnificent detachment: 'When I have disposed of my cloak, Doctor, I will accompany you round the ward.'

Shaun gave a sudden cry of impatience.

'Good God, woman!' he almost shouted. 'Why don't you call it an "outer garment" and have done with it?'

And, revealing exasperation for the first time since they had met, he stalked off.

But he was waiting outside the general ward when she was ready. Brisk, impersonal, he was no longer Shaun O'Hara, but Doctor O'Hara, interested in no one but his patients.

Oddly, ridiculously, Janet felt shut out. Forgotten. She thought: Nothing he ever says off duty means a thing. He is insincere, a flirt, nothing more than that . . . And, what was even more ridiculous, the thought depressed her.

'Ready, Sister?'

He opened the door for her to pass through. Unlike many doctors on the wards, he was always courteous. She had yet to hear him speak rudely to any member of the staff. She had even seen him step aside one morning to allow a cleaner to pass, a thing Phillip would never have done. Phillip was, perhaps, too conscious of his position, too much aware of seniority in rank. Such things meant little to Doctor O'Hara. A human being was a human being to him, be it a senior member of the medical staff, a patient, or the most menial hospital employee. She liked him for that.

The fact that she could even confess a liking for anything about Shaun surprised her. She had been at great pains to deny any likeable quality in him, ever since he had entered the ward kitchen and listened to her conversation with Linda, but now she wondered whether she had not been a little hasty in her judgment of him.

As always, as they moved from bed to bed she was aware of a deep admiration for the man at his work. Unlike Doctor Heron, he made his tour of the ward both interesting and instructive, not a duty to be discharged as quickly as possible. Everyone said that—in Raleigh and Drake, on Hood and Rodney and Beatty—and Linda had told her how highly he was already regarded in the path. lab.

When the round was completed Janet made her way to Richard Herrick's bed. This was a good opportunity to have a word with him. Somehow she felt it important to do so. The ward was quiet; many of the patients were already drowsy. Soon the lights would be turned off and the hush which fell upon the hospital at this hour would descend like an enveloping mantle.

She said: 'Comfortable, Dick?' Everyone called the boy by his Christian name, even though his father was chairman of the hospital. Dick Herrick had a simplicity and friendliness which made everyone—shipmates or hospital staff—feel that he was one of them.

'Fine,' she heard him say, but she was only half listening, for she was wondering how to introduce the subject which engrossed her mind.

'Tomorrow will be your great day,' she told him. 'You have been patient and brave . . .'

'No braver than any of the other fellows here. As for patience, how about old Perky over there?'

She smiled across the ward at the ex-seaman-gunner.

'Oh, he is part of the place,' she said fondly. 'I believe it will break my heart to see him go . . .' She hesitated, then went on: 'And talking of breaking hearts, I am worried about someone—'

'Another patient?' he asked.

157

'No. One of my nurses. One of whom I am particularly fond. So, I think, are you.'

He smiled. A tender, proud smile, she thought.

'Ah—you mean Nurse Watling.'

'Then you do care for her, Dick?'

'That seems a very inadequate way of expressing it.'

'You love her?'

'Yes.' He said the word with beautiful simplicity, acknowledging a truth which could never be changed. She felt a sudden constriction in her throat. It must be rather wonderful to be loved like that—with integrity and reverence. Integrity? That had yet to be put to the test.

He gave a sudden smile; a mischievous smile.

'Falling in love with one of the nurses isn't against the hospital rules, is it?' he teased.

'If it were, could rules and regulations control the heart? Of course, patients *have* thought the same thing before . . .'

'And found, when they got outside, that they had made a mistake?' He shook his head. 'There can be no mistake about this. I have even told my people—that is how sure I am.'

'And what did they say about it?'

'What any parents say to their son when they know he has found the right girl.'

Her hand fell upon his, briefly, gratefully.

'You'll be good to her, Dick?'

158

'Naturally!' He sounded surprised, a little annoyed that such a thing could be questioned.

'She has suffered a lot, that is why I ask.'

'I know.' He turned his shaded eyes toward Janet and said bluntly: 'Stop worrying, will you? I love Meg, and when you love a person you take darned good care not to hurt them. What do you think I am going to do? Turn away in horror when I set eyes on her?'

Janet gave a little gasp.

'Then she has told you!'

'No. She didn't tell me. I think she was too scared. And because I knew she was scared, I didn't let on that I knew.'

'Then you should have!' Janet retorted crossly. 'Meg is even more afraid now, as a result!'

'Afraid of me?' he asked incredulously.

'Afraid of experiencing something which happened once before—but this time I think it would hurt her even more.'

He was silent for a moment.

'Is she still in the ward? Could I have word with her—just for a minute or two?'

'The day staff has gone off duty. You will have to wait until tomorrow, young man. And so, poor mite, must she. Still,' Janet added with brisk satisfaction, 'love has abiding qualities. It will keep just as well until the morning!'

And, with a gentle laugh, she turned to leave the ward.

159

And found Shaun O'Hara waiting at her side.

They left the ward together. Outside, he said: 'So even you believe that love has abiding qualities—yet you are too afraid to put it to the test.'

'Afraid!' she echoed indignantly.

'Afraid of letting yourself fall in love—really in love.' His eyes and voice were serious now. 'Youngsters like Herrick and the Watling child can do it—even she, who has more reason to be frightened than you. They say suffering gives courage—perhaps it does. Doesn't nursing give courage, also? I should have expected it to.'

She made no answer. They stood alone in the deserted corridor. From the ward kitchen came the hum of voices, the clatter of crockery.

'Oh, Janet—*Janet!*' Shaun whispered urgently. 'Wake up before it is too late!'

She wanted to leave him, and could not. She ought to push open the swinging door leading to the kitchen and set about her duties, briskly. She ought to check the drug book—it was her responsibility to allocate sleeping pills to patients who needed them, and to see that no nurse administered drugs to patients who should now be sleeping naturally. She ought, she really *ought*, to push Shaun O'Hara on one side, finally and forever.

She gave a little sob and the sound surprised

160

even herself.

'Please go—oh, please go, Shaun!'

His dark, serious face lightened with a sudden smile.

'You called me by my Christian name! Did you mean to, Janet?'

She tried to step aside, but he waylaid her.

He said softly: 'You *are* in love, you know—and with me.'

She took a deep breath. It was ridiculous to tremble so. Dangerous, too. It weakened one's defenses. Besides, if anyone should come along, if any of the nurses should suddenly emerge from the ward kitchen, a pretty fool she would look standing in an empty corridor, blushing and trembling because one of the doctors was talking to her! They would hurry back to tell the other girls—to giggle and speculate and say: 'Poor old Humphrey! Fancy falling for one of the medics at *her* age . . .' And they would be right. To allow her heart to be captured by an impecunious doctor who still had his way to make in the world would be nothing short of disastrous. It was time to begin to plan one's life when one reached the disturbing age of nearly twenty-nine . . .

Shaun's voice continued with urgent pleading: 'Didn't you feel it too, that very first moment we met? I pushed open that door and there you were—trying so hard not to cry. That's the truth of it, isn't it now? Trying so hard, you were, to be happy and gay about

161

something which gave you no more thrill than a business appointment—and worrying you were, bless you, about facing a solitary old age!' His hands fell upon her shoulders. He shook her gently. 'There'll be no solitary old age for you, Janet, if you will be courageous enough to take what life has in store for you. It's no use trying to arrange it. Love doesn't come that way!'

He put one finger beneath her chin and tilted her face upwards.

'You know,' he continued, 'it would be almost funny if it weren't so pathetic, this engagement of yours to a man like Bailey. I looked at you both the other night, across that dining-room, and you looked like a couple who had done the same thing for years and were too caught up by the habit to realize the monotony of it! And I thought: *That* is what their marriage would be like—if it were ever allowed to take place! He would bore you, Janet! Because you are not in love with him and never have been—and if you don't tell him, I will.'

'Let me go! *Let me go!*'

'And why should I be letting you go? Why should you be running away?'

She said desperately: 'I would like to be alone, Shaun!' and meant it. She wanted to think. To think and think and get things clear. She wanted to tear the mists of pretense from her heart and look into it, frankly. She wanted

162

to find out why, deep within her, something stirred with a sweetness more exquisite than she had ever known; something trembled and came to life, like a butterfly emerging from its chrysalis. Something which had lain dormant all her life struggled to awake.

He dropped a gentle kiss upon her brow. Thank God, she thought, for this precious seclusion! She prayed no one would invade it. As if sensing her thoughts, Shaun said gently: 'Don't worry. You know no one will come along at this hour. You know all the duties your nurses are engaged upon right now—they would be too scared to be found in one of the corridors when they should be elsewhere—but I am going, Janet. I ask only one thing—'

'What is it?'

'That you'll be remembering what I've said—and thinking about it.'

'I'll remember.'

How could she do otherwise? How could she prevent his voice from echoing in her memory like a tune she could not suppress?

'One day,' he said, and the tenderness in his voice was a caress, 'one day I'll be taking you back to Killarney, and you'll meet my parents, safe and happy in their Irish dell. And you'll be looking at your own old age and yourself as you'll be forty years from now. And you'll recall what you said to that boy—that love has abiding qualities . . .'

CHAPTER TWENTY

When Linda entered the laboratory she saw what she had expected to see—Brett's fair head stooped above his work. Intent, absorbed, he did not hear her. She crossed the room, her crêpe-soled hospital shoes soundless upon the rubber floor, and as she did so that sixth sense, which always told him of her presence, made him turn.

Caught off guard, his reaction was revealing.

'Linda!'

The glad surprise in his voice was unmistakable, but in a second he had suppressed it.

'What are you doing here?' he asked.

'I saw your light from the window of my room. I came to see if I could help.'

'No need,' he told her abruptly. 'I can finish this job.'

'Two could finish it more quickly than one,' she said calmly, and took some of the graphs he was working upon. Routine stuff, she thought. This could have waited until tomorow. Did the man live for his laboratory? Did he think of nothing but work?

'I presumed you were working on that serum for Doctor Chambers?'

'Finished that,' he muttered, and turned

164

away.

But his face still wore that betraying flush, and she could still hear that tell-tale gladness in his voice. The memory of it warmed her heart and gave her courage to say: 'I don't suppose you have eaten. When these are done, shall we go out and have something? I would get something from the cafeteria, but they are closed at this hour.'

'There's no need,' he said. 'I'll eat when I get back to my flat.'

Linda checked a smile. That was meant as a snub, she thought, but I'm not going to take it.

'We could go to Mike's Place,' she said gently.

Silence. He turned and looked at her. She was sitting at her own table, apparently intent upon her graph. He answered gruffly: 'If you like.'

'I'd like to very much,' she told him lightly.

Silence again.

'We should be through these by nine o'clock,' Linda continued. 'They stay open quite late, don't they?'

'Yes. We can get a meal there any time up to eleven.'

She smiled at him over her shoulder and continued with her work. Nothing more was said for a few minutes. The laboratory was very quiet. Only a tap dripping into a distant sink and the occasional stirring of a guinea pig in its sleep disturbed the moment. She heard

165

Brett move restlessly upon his high stool. Outside, an ambulance clanged its bell as the first night casualty arrived. Linda looked across at the frosted windows of the operating theatre, which faced the laboratory across a dividing well.

His voice came across the room again.

'No engagement tonight, Linda?'

'No.' She added with a smile: 'I don't go out every evening, you know.'

Brett looked surprised—so surprised that she laughed.

'Good gracious, you don't imagine my life is one long social round, do you?'

'No—not exactly.'

'Heaven help my work, if it were!'

She stooped above her table again. He looked at her for a long moment, thoughtfully. She knew quite well that he was looking at her and, for this reason, averted her face. Sometimes she could not look at Brett squarely, lest her eyes betray her.

But she managed to keep that cool, impersonal note in her voice as she asked: 'Why did you leave Andrew's party so early?'

He shrugged.

'Parties aren't in my line.'

'Isn't that rather an unsociable attitude?'

'Not really. It's just that I don't fit. Crowds make me dry up conversationally.'

'You seemed to be getting on well with my father. I saw you talking to him very earnestly

166

when I entered.'

He evaded that. No doubt her father had repeated his remarks, and a fine fool that had made him appear in her eyes. The thought filled him with embarrassment.

'What were you talking about?' she asked.

'Didn't he tell you?'

'Not a thing. Father's funny that way. He will only part with information voluntarily, so I never try to pump him. Besides, Aunt Ethel barged in. You haven't met my Aunt Ethel, have you?' He shook his head, and Linda laughed. 'She's all right—in small doses. She's sure to be at the hospital ball next week; Mother and Father always include her in their party. You'll meet her then.'

'I shan't be there.'

'Not there!' Dismay broke through her guard. 'Oh, but you *must*!'

'Why?'

'I—we'd all like you to come, of course. Besides, everyone will be there . . .'

He put the last graph aside, stepped down from his stool and strolled across the laboratory to wash his hands. Above the sound of gushing water he said: 'I've told you, I'm no good at social functions. As for dancing, I've never learned how to.'

'Only because you've had little opportunity, perhaps. But at these hospital dances no one is frightfully particular—we don't condemn our partners because they are not experts! Do come, Brett—'

She rarely used his Christian name, but she uttered it now quite naturally. He looked at her—at her heart-shaped face framed in its dark hair. He loved the way she dressed it, coiled at the nape of her neck and smooth on top; no untidy ends; no fluffy little curls. Linda wasn't the fluffy type. She was streamlined and shining—that was how he thought of her. Long and slender and flawlessly groomed from the top of her glossy head to the tips of her neatly shod feet. She always dressed simply, without ostentation, and as a result possessed a distinction which other girls envied. She was never a slave to fashion, following blindly the hair stylists or the dress designers' whims, but was always essentially individual.

The way she wore her hair, he thought, was characteristic of her. Sometimes he wanted to put out his hand and stroke the soft sleekness of it. He knew what it would feel like—the petals of a tulip. One of those dark, glossy tulips which stood out so richly, so warmly in any flower garden. Yes, he thought, that is what she reminds me of—a black tulip.

He said abruptly: 'Put that stuff aside, Linda, and let's go.'

Willingly, she obeyed.

'You'd better let the home orderly know you are going to be late,' he reminded her.

Linda smiled. 'I have already done so!'

They walked through the cobbled streets

skirting the harbor, and the smell of the sea came to them like the tang of spices in the air. Above, stars hung in the black canopy of the sky like sequins flung by a graceful hand. The breezes were salty and strong, wafting inland the smell of tar, the smell of ships, the smell of far-away places . . .

Linda looked out across the inky sea and said dreamily: 'I love this old town. I love this harbor. I love its swashbuckling air of adventure . . .'

Brett looked at her in surprise, for he had never seen this side to her nature—only the cool, poised young woman who worked in the laboratory and disturbed him with her nearness. He had never suspected an underlying wistfulness, a romanticism, but it was there now—in her voice and in her starry eyes as they looked heavenwards.

'Just think,' she whispered, 'the wind that is touching us at this moment was touching some distant land only a short while ago . . .'

He said wonderingly: 'I never knew you felt this way about Rockport'—and he marvelled a little because, so often, he had felt this way himself.

Linda answered gently: 'How do you know how I feel about anything?'

In the moonlight her lovely eyes met his, almost with a look of challenge. Then she gave a half-amused, half-angry little laugh.

'Why, you don't know me at all!' she cried.

He heard himself saying: 'But I should like to . . .' and was immediately amazed at his own temerity. It was not his habit to expose his heart, and he felt now that he had revealed its innermost depths to her. He was grateful for the darkness which concealed his embarrassment.

Linda whispered softly: 'Then why don't you, Brett?'

CHAPTER TWENTY-ONE

The hospital secretary arrived promptly at nine each morning. Knowing this, Janet went straight to his office, as she came off duty, and waited for him. He was pleased to see her, but surprised.

'Ah, Janet,' he said, as he hung his hat upon its peg and placed his neatly rolled umbrella in its stand. With meticulous, unhurried movements he shed his overcoat, placed his gloves neatly in one pocket, and hung that up, too. Then he crossed to her, saying:

'This is a nice surprise, my dear. Do you wish to speak to me about something?'

She stared at him in astonishment. She might have been there by appointment upon some business matter. Was he always like this, in his office? Did he never relax—even before work began? She had expected a display of pleasant surprise, not this cool, matter-of-fact acceptance. Well, perhaps it was a good thing. Perhaps it would be easier to tell him what she had come to tell him.

'Sit down, my dear—'

'I am only staying a moment, Phillip—'

'I'm afraid that is all I can spare, Janet.' He made a vague gesture with his hand towards his desk. 'Work, you know, must begin promptly. Which reminds me—' He glanced at his watch. 'My secretary is late!'

'She is in the outer office. I asked if I could speak to you alone.'

His eyebrows went up.

'You need not have done that,' he said. 'Miss Brown knows all the affairs of this hospital. I discuss everything in front of her.'

'But I don't want to speak to you about the hospital, Phillip. I had to seek you here because, being on night duty, I can't see you after office hours.'

'Of course, my dear—' And, apologetically, he kissed her cheek. Sensing her withdrawal, he looked at her and said sharply: 'What is the matter? Why have you come to see me?'

'To ask you to accept this, Phillip—'

She tried to keep her voice steady as she held out the shabby little jewel box, but the moment was not easy. She had not expected it to be easy. She had come to a decision during the long, quiet hours of the night—an uneventful night it had been, bringing no distractions to take her mind off her own affairs; a night which gave her plenty of time in which to think, to look at things squarely, to be honest with herself. After that, there had been no question about what she must do. There was only one decision, and she had made it. And she knew that it was right.

Phillip gave a swift frown.

'What is this, my dear—a joke?' And then with an air of relief, he exclaimed: 'Of course! You want the ring made smaller, is that it? You know, my dear, for one moment I thought you were giving it back to me!' He gave a thin laugh.

'I am giving it back to you, Phillip. Please understand—and forgive me—but I cannot marry you.'

'*Cannot!*' His sharp face tautened. 'You don't mean this, Janet!'

She said gently: 'I'm afraid I do. You see, I don't love you. I never have loved you. All I can give you is liking and a very sincere friendship. That isn't enough for marriage.'

'It is enough for me. I have never asked more of you.'

'But it can't be enough! A marriage without love would be terrible! I should have realized that before.'

'You certainly should!' he answered tartly, then looked at her in swift suspicion. 'Who has been talking to you? Who put these ideas into your head? You're not a sentimental

172

schoolgirl, Janet. You're level-headed and sane and would make me a very good wife—as I,' he added hastily, 'would make you a very good husband.'

'But I don't want a husband I cannot love.'

With admirable control he answered: 'You're tired, my dear. Night duty has placed a strain upon you—'

'Not in the least, Phillip. Please, take this!'

But still he did not.

'It is yours,' he answered frigidly. 'I gave it to you and I command you to wear it.'

'Command?'

'Most definitely. I have not the slightest intention of allowing you to break our engagement. What sort of a fool would that make me appear in the eyes of the hospital?' He uttered a short, disgusted sound. 'Jilted! *That* is what they would call it!' His voice rose angrily. She had never heard it raised before, and the realization that it could actually do so came to Janet with a sense of surprise. 'Oh no, my dear girl, you don't do such a thing to me! I'll not be made a laughingstock. I'll not have my position here subjected to such indignity!'

'So that is what you are worrying about—your position!'

'And why not? It is an important position, a respected one.' He gave her a sudden shrewd look. 'Are you in love with someone else—or imagining yourself to be?'

She answered truthfully: 'I don't know, but I

do know that I don't love you and that I cannot marry you in such circumstances. I did wrong when I agreed to marry you, and for that I ask you to forgive me, but I didn't see it like this at the time. Now I know it would not be fair to you. I would make you miserable.'

'Nonsense. I have never been miserable with you, Janet, so why should I suddenly start to be?' His anger was under control now. He said with elaborate patience: 'Now run along and get some sleep and we'll forget this interview,' but he said it with such a tone of magnanimity that it was Janet who became angry.

'I'll do nothing of the sort, Phillip, and I refuse to be ordered about like a child! Please understand—I am not going to marry you!'

He took a step toward her. Behind his pale-rimmed spectacles his eyes had narrowed, and when he came close she saw that his nostrils were dilated. She felt a swift alarm. She had never seen Phillip look like this. But he wasn't going to frighten her into submission, on that she was determined.

She held out the jewel box again.

'I have asked you to take this, Phillip.'

When he made no movement, she placed the ring upon his desk and turned to go. Immediately, his hands shot out and gripped her shoulders. His thin fingers were surprisingly strong, pressing into her flesh even through the thick material of her uniform. He

174

shook her—swiftly and viciously—then, horrified at what he had done, stepped back. The abrupt release sent Janet stumbling against his desk. She gripped it to steady herself and remained there, leaning against it, while she regained her breath. And Phillip faced her, coldly furious. He was trembling and fighting for control.

'Who is it? Who is responsible? Who are you in love with?'

Janet smoothed her uniform and straightened her cuffs. She regarded him coolly, even though pain stabbed her shoulders.

'Isn't it sufficient that I cannot marry you? Must there be any other reason than the one I have given you—the only real and truthful one? I have been thinking very seriously during the night. I have analyzed my feelings very frankly. I am not breaking our engagement because I want to marry someone else, but simply because I know I cannot marry you.'

Again she turned toward the door, and again Phillip stopped her. This time, however, he did not touch her, but placed himself deliberately in her path. He was no longer the urbane hospital secretary, but a man enraged to the point of hatred.

'If any man in this hospital has come between us,' he said in a quiet, deadly voice, 'I shall do my best to get him dismissed. And,' he added smoothly, 'I think you will agree that a man in my position can do a lot to undermine the position of others . . .'

She looked at him with a faint curl of contempt upon her lips, and the sight of it goaded him further.

'Is it O'Hara?' he demanded. 'I've observed that vulgar Irishman hanging around Cunningham Ward rather a lot. Far more than Doctor Heron ever did!'

'Doctor O'Hara visits all the wards far more than Doctor Heron ever did.'

'Are you in love with the man?' The well-controlled, pedantic voice was now completely out of hand. 'Are you bewitched by his romantic good looks and his Irish brogue and his flattery? If so, you're making a fool of yourself, my girl! It must be your age! I've heard that as a woman approaches thirty she is prone to make a fool of herself over any handsome face—'

'Rubbish!' said a voice.

It belonged to Shaun.

He stood with his back to the door, leaning against it.

'I thought you would be here, Janet. I had an idea you would call upon Augustus as you came off duty. I came down to support you and believed I was in time. Did you leave the ward early?'

'Yes,' Janet whispered. 'It was not a busy night.'

176

Shaun strolled into the room, first opening the door and leaving it ajar.

'Are you wanting to leave, Janet?' he said gently. 'If so, the way is now clear . . .'

She did not move.

Phillip's small eyes darted from one to the other suspiciously.

'There's something going on between you two,' he said truculently.

'Why did you come, Shaun?' Janet asked.

He gave her a tender smile.

'You don't think I would leave you to face Augustus alone, do you?'

'Mr. Bailey, to you,' said Phillip.

But Shaun ignored him. His voice continued quietly: 'I don't like to see women hurt, or hear them abused. Besides, Augustus, I have something to tell you. I am in love with Janet. More than "in love" with her. I want to marry her.'

'I knew it! You lied to me, Janet!'

'Oh no, she didn't! The trouble is that Janet won't realize she loves me. In fact, she insists, even to herself, that she does not. But she will come around to it in time,' Shaun smiled. 'And so *you* will, Augustus. And when you do, you will be thankful you didn't imperil your precious position by marrying a girl who might have involved you in some scandal later on—'

'Scandal!' Augustus echoed distastefully. 'What sort of scandal?' 'The very worst,' Shaun answered gravely.

The hospital secretary gave a contemptuous laugh. 'Janet would never be involved in any sort of scandal.

She was far too respectably brought up.'

'Just the type to go to the other extreme. Believe me, you've had a narrow escape, Augustus! If Janet had married you she'd have upped and thrown her cap high over the windmill—very high indeed. Of course,' he finished calmly, 'I would have been there to catch it . . .'

'What are you talking about?' Bailey demanded frigidly.

'Her nose, Augustus. It should have warned you.'

'Have you been drinking?'

'At nine in the morning? Augustus, where's your sense of humor?'

Janet stifled a laugh, and Augustus surveyed her with doubt and disapproval. Her high-handed rejection of himself now suggested alarming possibilities, chief among them being the possibility that O'Hara was right about her. After all, he was obviously a man who knew women; a rake who recognized the feminine counterpart of himself, however respectably disguised . . .

It might be true, indeed, that he had had a narrow escape!

Shaun placed a hand beneath Janet's elbow and led her to the door. She paused and looked back.

178

'If it would help your pride, Phillip, you could tell everyone that you broke the engagement—not I.'

'I most certainly shall.'

Shaun chuckled.

'Then everyone can say I caught you on the rebound, Janet—and so long as I do catch you, that way is as good as any!'

But the secretary-superintendent of the Royal Rockport Hospital could not resist a final taunt.

'You may have heard me warning Janet just now that I would ruin any man who took her from me, O'Hara, and although I no longer consider that she would make a good wife I still intend to do my best to get rid of you. I have never considered you the right type of doctor for this hospital.'

Shaun surveyed him with contemptuous amusement.

'Go ahead, Augustus, and do your damnedest! But let me remind you that, despite your inflated awareness of position, you have no influence at all where medical appointments are concerned. Try to make mischief if you like, but if a doctor's work is satisfactory that won't get you very far.'

He shut the door. He looked down at Janet with whimsical tenderness. He said: 'This is one engagement you're not having time to consider, my darling. I'm carrying you off as soon as I get a special license. Of course, we have another date before that—'

Janet felt the strong, reassuring touch of his hand, saw the kind, humorous light in his eye, and suddenly her heart was at peace. Suddenly she was soaring to the stars . . .

'Another date, Shaun? For what?'

'To find a ruby—warm and vital as yourself. The loveliest ruby I can buy—even if I have to embezzle the hospital funds to buy it!'

They laughed together, united in happiness, and as they walked on Shaun whispered: 'It's a pity these hospital corridors offer no more privacy at nine in the morning than Piccadilly Circus at midday—otherwise I'd be kissing you, Janet Humphrey, and by all the Saints of Ireland, you'd be liking it!'

CHAPTER TWENTY-TWO

Emerging from the dispensary with the morning dressing-basket, Meg came face to face with Janet. Despite the tension which gripped her, Meg could not fail to observe Nurse Humphrey's radiance. She looked as if she had just reached up and touched the stars.

She was with that nice Doctor O'Hara and, from the looks of things, they were too absorbed in one another to notice anyone else. Therefore Meg hurried by, and not until she had gone did Janet realize that she had missed an opportunity to comfort and reassure the child.

'Oh, Shaun—how could I have been so blind! And I can't go on to the ward after her, now that I am off duty . . .'

'I'd like to see Sister Marlow's face if you dared to intrude on her domain after your reign had finished,' said Shaun. 'Which reminds me, I'm on duty in five minutes, and if I want to land the senior physician's appointment which, McNeil told me yesterday, will become vacant next year, I'd better be going. And,' he finished, 'I'm going to land it Janet.'

He gave her hand a brief farewell pressure, which was all he dared steal at this moment.

'Let me have an hour alone with you, Janet, before you go on duty tonight. I want to hear you say something . . .'

She smiled at him tremulously, knowing what he meant.

'I could say it now, Shaun,' she whispered. And did so. She murmured the words as if they were a prayer, and never had they sounded more wonderful to any man.

Sleep, of course, was out of the question. She was too excited, too wildly happy, dizzy with ecstasy. Never had she felt like this before. Never had her heart felt so full—nor so free. It was like a bird which had escaped from a long and lonely imprisonment and now flew straight toward the sun. And in the center of that brilliant orbit shone the face of Shaun O'Hara—proud and conquering, tender and passionate. And so infinitely dear . . .

Her feet, too, had wings as she stepped out across the courtyard towards the nurses' home. Linda, whose laboratory duties began at half past nine, met her at the entrance and stood still.

'Something has happened,' she said, staring at her friend and thinking that without a doubt happiness was the greatest beautifier in the world.

Janet gave a gay, excited laugh.

'You always know, don't you, Linda?'

'Looking at you, the whole world must know. Tell me—'

But Janet shook her head.

'Too many nurses around, Linda, and my news is too precious to be bandied all over the hospital—yet. But I promise you this—when the time comes, you will be the first to hear.'

Linda's warm smile flashed out.

'Fair enough,' she agreed. 'Whatever it is, I'm glad about it. And,' she added, 'I hope it is what I think it is . . .'

Janet laughed.

'You could be right!' she said.

'As right as the whole world is for you, at this moment?'

'As right as it is going to be for Meg, too. I had a talk with Richard Herrick last night. Linda, he knows! He has known all along!'

'Oh, Janet—if only we could have told her that!'

'That is what I was thinking a moment ago. But now I'm not so sure. Won't it be more wonderful for her to find out for herself?'

Yes, thought Linda happily, undoubtedly it would be. She went on her way, contented because Janet's world had, in the only possible way, suddenly righted itself. Which means, thought Linda, that either she has fallen out of love with Augustus (if she was ever in it) or *in* love with Shaun (if she was ever out of it) and if that doesn't make sense to the rest of the world, at least it does to me!

As she entered the hospital she glanced down the corridor leading to Cunningham Ward. Was Meg—tense and anxious—even now approaching Richard's bed? Was the curtain about to rise on her happiness, too? It seemed so. It seemed that life, after all, might have much in store for Meg, and if anyone deserved so rich a reward, it was she.

There's certainly a God in His Heaven, thought Linda gratefully, and right at this moment He seems pretty busy. It must be a nice feeling, having the power to bring happiness to people . . . would it be very selfish of me to ask for a little, too?

CHAPTER TWENTY-THREE

Contrary to all their expectations, Meg had no opportunity to enter the main ward in Cunningham that morning. She was kept busy in the private wards and the kitchen, and after lunch there was an hour's lecture to attend. She returned to duty just when visiting hours were about to begin—and came face to face with Shirley Travers.

Armed with gifts, Shirley was going into the waiting-room at the end of the corridor. Meg knew her by sight. Everyone in Rockport did. Besides, she had good reason to be aware of Shirley's pretty face. It gave her a shock to see her, but the shock bore no pain of reminder— all that, she knew, was gone. Finished with. What Shirley did or what Keith had done no longer mattered. Indeed, since she became a nurse at the Royal Rockport Hospital Meg had scarcely given either either of them a thought.

The shock was because she had learned that Shirley had come to visit Richard. A fellow student nurse told her. 'She's an old flame of his, didn't you know?' Hunter loved a bit of gossip. 'My sister—she's a hair-dresser, you know, down at Alphonse's salon in the Square—well, Alphonse (his name's Bert Smith, really!) often sends his assistants to clients' homes, and my sister goes to the

Travers' every now and then. Old Mrs. Travers has had her hair *dyed*, my dear, at sixty! Of course Vi (that's my sister) always hears what's going on when she has tea afterwards with the housekeeper. She's a mine of information, that woman, and did they laugh when Shirley didn't pull it off!'

'Pull what off?' murmured Meg.

'Why, marrying Richard Herrick, of course! Dead set on him, she was—and still is, I wouldn't be surprised! Vi says Mrs. Diddams (she's the housekeeper) says that Shirley only took the Saunders boy because she couldn't get Richard Herrick—Why, what's the matter?'

'Nothing. Go on—'

'You looked so startled—well, that's all, really. Except that it seems she hasn't given up hope, after all. She's being awfully stubborn this afternoon, too—refuses to go away this time. Oh no, my dear, it isn't the first time she's been—when he first arrived she was calling every day, but he wouldn't see anyone except his parents. They are with him now, and my word, don't they look happy! There were tears in Lady Herrick's eyes when I went in to collect the water carafes. It must be an awful relief to them to know that he can see all right. I say, Watling, be a sport and sterilize these specimen glasses for me, will you?'

'All right,' Meg agreed absently. 'Tell me— has he finished with the shield? Isn't he

185

wearing it now?'

'Finished with it altogether! Isn't it wonderful?'

'More than wonderful . . .'

'All credit to Mr. McNeil—he's a marvel, that man!'

Aware of a perilous lump in her throat, Meg turned away. So it was nearly over, she thought, and it would be over completely before long. The sooner the better, perhaps. She knew a sense of relief and gratitude because Richard's sight was insured, but a sense of loss because she could no longer be of use to him. She had served her purpose. She had given him faith and encouragement and hope, so perhaps her deception had been worth while. Perhaps, too, he would not feel too great a disappointment when he found out, especially if he could turn from her and look upon someone as pretty as Shirley Travers. How conveniently the girl had timed her arrival—almost as if she had known, or the powers-that-be had arranged it!

But it was cruel, bitterly cruel that whenever she herself was threatened with loss, Shirley should be at hand to gain by it . . .

Meg made a valiant effort to pull herself together. Ever since her accident she had fought and conquered the danger of self-pity. She had, she insisted, no reason to feel sorry for herself—indeed, she had every reason to feel otherwise, for the future held more than hope. The future was in the skilled hands of Simon Wardour, and although Meg knew nothing about him, she felt an instinctive confidence in the man.

Whatever happened now, whatever life might deny her, she could at least count upon that. Her face would be made whole again. She would no longer bear the burden of self-consciousness, nor face the humiliation of pity. She could lift her head and look the world in the face.

But if only Richard did not have to see her before that!

The staff nurse who had temporarily replaced Janet on day duty said sharply: 'Get on with the tea-trays now, Watling—there's only another thirty minutes before visiting time finishes, and the patients will be clamoring for their tea by that time. You can take the trays round the main ward and you—what's your name? Hunter?—you can do the isolations . . .'

The door swung open abruptly. Sister Marlow stood there. She beckoned Meg with an imperative finger, and the staff nurse uttered an impatient sigh as Meg disappeared. Now the teas would be later than ever, she grumbled, unless she herself gave a hand. Still grumbling, she descended from her senior perch and began to spread jam upon slices of buttered bread as if (said Hunter afterwards) she was an angry barber lathering a victim's face . . .

Sister Marlow said: 'Lady Herrick wishes to speak to you, Nurse,' and, inclining her head with deferential dignity toward the quiet, grey-haired lady who stood beside her, she disappeared into her sanctum.

Richard's mother was small and plump and maternal. She had a sweet, friendly face and a manner which put people immediately at ease. She held out her hand and said: 'So you are Meg—Richard has told us all about you . . .'

'All about me?' echoed Meg.

'All that you have done for him, and all that you mean to him, my dear.' She placed her hands upon Meg's shoulders and, drawing near, kissed her gently upon the cheek. 'I'm not good at making speeches and my husband declares I will never learn, but perhaps it is enough, at this moment, to say: "Thank you, my dear . . ."'

'There is nothing to thank me for!'

'On the contrary, Richard's father and I both feel we owe you more than we can ever repay. But for you—' The soft voice broke. 'You gave him faith, child. I even believe you gave him more than that . . .'

Touching Meg's arm, she turned toward the ward.

'Come, my dear, he is waiting for you—'

Meg shrank.

'Come,' the quiet voice insisted. 'My son wants to see you.'

188

'No—no! He mustn't!'

'He must—he shall,' said Richard's mother, and opened the door on to the ward.

Meg walked through it. She walked beside Lady Herrick to the distant bed where Richard awaited her. There were screens round it, to cut off the direct light from the window, and when—moving like an automaton—Meg stepped beyond them, she saw that Richard was not in bed, but sitting in an arm-chair, wearing a dressing-gown. There was a green shade above his eyes, but it could not conceal their amazing blueness, and she thought in a remote part of her mind: I knew he would have the eyes of a sailor . . .

His father stood beside him, one hand upon his shoulder—a tall, upright figure of a man with the same blue eyes and the same firm mouth. When Meg appeared he stepped aside and waited.

Meg felt a woman's hand drawing her forward.

'She is here, Dick,' said his mother gently.

Richard turned his head, and looked at Meg.

They looked at one another for a long moment. A clear, revealing moment which trembled like a crystal suspended from heaven. Unaware that her wounded young face wore a smile so tender that it eclipsed all ugliness and brought tears to the eyes of Richard's mother, and a sudden lump to the throat of his father,

Meg stood still—waiting.

Richard spoke her name very quietly. Something in his voice made her heart tremble like the beat of urgent wings within her breast.

He put out his hands and drew her toward him.

'Stoop down, Meg,' he commanded softly, and when she obeyed he lifted his face and kissed her wounded cheek.

When he withdrew, her tears lay upon his lips.

'Why did you do that?' she whispered.

'Because I love you.'

'Not because you pity me, Richard?'

'Because I love you, just as you are. I haven't pitied you all along, Meg, so why should I do so now?'

'But you didn't *know*—then.'

'Of course I did!' Still holding her hands, he shook them gently. 'When a man is blind, my darling, his fingers become his eyes. He can visualize, through touch, many unsuspected things. The moment I touched this poor cheek of yours, I knew.'

'And it made no difference!'

'Only to make me love you more, if that were possible.'

She sobbed. Above her and around her the heavens sang and through the floodgates of her heart happiness poured in a glad, tumultuous torrent.

'Oh, Richard—*Richard!*' she whispered

brokenly, forgetful of the world behind the screen, forgetful of ears that might hear and eyes that might see, forgetful of everyone and everything but the wonder of this moment. 'I shall not look like this forever! I shall be cured—*cured*, Richard! And soon! A man named Simon Wardour is going to give me treatment. I've agreed to let him practice on me and he is quite confident that he can *cure*—Why, what is the matter?'

She broke off, for Richard had subsided into laughter. His frank, boyish face regarded her with tender amusement.

'Wardour!' he choked. *'Wardour wants practice?'*

'That is what he said,' Meg answered, bewildered.

'My sweet, do you realize he is the most brilliant plastic surgeon in England?'

'He can't be! Not that ordinary little man?'

'Yes—that ordinary little man. I'm not making any mistake, Meg—ask Dad here. He knows him well, don't you—?'

But they were alone. And how long they had been alone, neither knew.

'Bless them!' said Richard fondly. 'They're a grand pair of parents, Meg. You'll love them— and they will certainly love you. Which reminds me—they visited your father yesterday. You didn't know that, did you? They went on my behalf and stayed on behalf of themselves . . .'

'On your behalf?' echoed Meg.

Richard gave her a teasing smile. 'I had to ask for your hand by proxy, darling. Somehow, I fancied my future father-in-law might like me better if I did. The parents thoroughly enjoyed themselves, I gather, talking roses, roses all the way!'

There was a sound beside them. Turning in unison, they looked at Shirley Travers. She gave Richard a dazzling smile, ignored Meg, and said: 'I saw your father and mother come out of the ward, Dick—so I came in. That waiting-room down the corridor is too tedious for words!'

She bestowed a brief glance upon Meg—a glance which spoke volumes. Why doesn't she go? it said. A nurse has no right to linger when a patient has visitors.

Richard placed his arm round Meg's waist. He held her close. Shirley's eyebrows went up.

'Really!' she exclaimed. 'I'm broadminded, Dick, but surely it isn't customary to flirt with the nurses so blatantly?'

Unexpectedly, it was Meg who answered. There was laughter in her voice, and a gaiety which she thought had died.

'As son of the hospital's chairman, Miss Travers, Mr. Herrick has certain privileges,' she said demurely.

Richard chuckled.

Shirley shrugged her elegant shoulders—blue fox and parma velvet enhanced by Chanel

No. 5. But her loveliness meant nothing to Richard, who surveyed her with an ironical smile and said: 'What Nurse Watling means, Shirley, is that I am to have the privilege of placing a ring upon her finger at the earliest opportunity.'

Shirley stiffened. Her cold, calculating little face hardened and she said shrilly: 'What are you talking about, Dick?'

'My engagement to Meg,' he said amiably. 'I'm sure you would like to be the first to congratulate us.'

'Meg?' echoed Shirley, on a taut, high note.

'Meg Watling,' said Richard. 'At present, that is.'

Shirley Travers uttered a stifled sound. For a moment she stood there, unable to control her fury. Then she spun upon her heel.

A moment later she turned back. She had laid a sheaf of expensive roses on Richard's bed and a box of precious cigarettes. Now she snatched them up and, sparing the couple not another glance, stalked off down the ward.

Richard said calmly: 'Before that interruption, my darling, I had been about to tell you that I'm glad to hear about Simon Wardour, but only for your sake. For my own, I love you as you are—and always will.'

The ward door swung open again and Hunter's brisk footsteps came hurrying down the ward.

'Where *has* Watling got to?' she demanded

of the room in general. 'The staff nurse will raise the dust if she isn't around to bring in the trays ...'

Perkins jerked his head toward the screen.

'In conference,' he informed her laconically, and turned back to his paper.

Hunter poked her head round a corner, and what she saw caused her to exclaim in horror: 'I say, you two, break it up! Sister might walk in!'

'She won't,' Richard told her, 'by special request. What's the use of having the chairman of this hospital for a father if a chap can't trade on it when necessary?'

But Meg hurried from the ward, too radiantly happy to feel guilty, but already too conscientious a nurse to shirk duty. And Perkins, seeing the happiness in her eyes, winked at her gaily and chirped:

'Everything ticketty-boo, Nurse? Thank Gawd for that! Now we can all relax, eh, fellers?'

CHAPTER TWENTY-FOUR

Brett Rogers had always believed that his comfortable bachelor flat lacked nothing. He had even believed that he wanted no more from life than his work, his books, and his own fireside, but this afternoon work had gone dead on him and, for the first time, he had left the laboratory early. Safe within the walls of his home (he believed) he would stop thinking about Linda and wondering why she had rushed out so suddenly in the middle of the morning—and failed to return.

Such behavior on the part of his reliable assistant was unprecedented—but not, it seemed, inexplicable. He had been down in the wards at the time, collecting clinical material, and when he returned it was to hear, from his lab. boy, that Miss Powell had received a telephone call and had promptly gone out.

'Seemed in an awful hurry, sir—just flung off her coverall and grabbed her coat and dashed off. Didn't even stop to say where she was going . . .'

There was her white coverall, sprawling over her stool, bearing evidence as to her taste.

Brett's immediate conclusion had been that an emergency in her home had called her away. Illness, perhaps. Not the old man, he hoped, for he had taken a great liking to Joseph Powell, even though he had made a fool of himself before him. But the lab. boy's next words dismissed that idea.

'It was Mr. McNeil who rang, sir.'

Brett could still feel the sharp ache of his disappointment . . .

'What makes you think that?'

'Well, sir, she seemed awfully excited.'

Brett frowned upon the boy.

'The mere fact that the senior visiting surgeon rings through to the laboratory, Tompkins, isn't necessarily a cause for excitement,' he answered stonily.

'No, sir—but he wasn't ringing the laboratory. He was ringing Miss Powell personally. I took the call, sir, and he asked for her.'

'And then?'

'Well, I couldn't hear what Mr. McNeil said, but I did hear what Miss Powell said . . .'

'And that was?'

'"Andrew, how wonderful!"' The boy cleared his throat. 'That was her, sir, using his Christian name—not me.'

'I know, I know,' said Brett impatiently. 'What then?'

'Then she said: "I'd *love* to come!" Just like that, sir. Then he said something, I don't know what, and she seemed awfully delighted, sir. She said: "Of course I'll come! I wouldn't miss it for the world!" Or something like that. Then she dropped the receiver back on its hook, flung off her coverall, and grabbed her coat—'

'And didn't she say where she was going?'

'Didn't say another word, sir. Seemed in too much of a hurry. So that's how I gathered,' said the lab. boy proudly, 'that Miss Powell was excited about something!'

'All right, Dick Barton—go along now and get on with your work.'

But Brett had been unable, after that, to get on with his own.

Work, books, and his own fireside—were these really enough for a man? It seemed not. Not even for one as self-sufficient and reserved as himself. His book—the third he had attempted to start this evening—now lay, forgotten, upon his lap. His fire was dying, and he could not be bothered restoking it. He had never felt so much alone.

So he can do that to her, he thought bitterly. Crook his little finger and set her running. One call from Andrew McNeil and she tossed her work aside and rushed to join him. Could anything be more eloquent than that?

The sudden buzz of his front-door bell startled Brett. He had few acquaintances outside the hospital and certainly no friends intimate enough to disturb his solitary evening. Beneath his depression he felt a stirring of curiosity and went to answer the summons, conscious of relief because his solitude had been invaded, even briefly.

Outside stood Linda's father.

His bright, friendly eyes twinkled as he said: 'Remember that beer you promised? I could drink it right now.'

Brett gave one of his rare smiles. It banished the stern lines about his mouth and the impression of taciturn unfriendliness which so often chilled people. He was delighted to see the old man—so delighted that he held the door wide and did not even remember how hurriedly he had fled from him last time they met.

Eagerly, he poked up the fire, fetched glasses and bottles. His gratitude for company, thought Joseph Powell, was almost pathetic—or would be, if it had been impossible for a man like Brett to make friends. But it was not impossible. All it needed was an understanding hand to pry open his shell.

Linda had tried, she said, and failed. But wasn't it probable that a man in love—a man as shy as Brett Rogers—might shrink from revealing his heart too plainly to the woman he loved? And taking into consideration all that Linda had told him, and the obvious signs he himself had observed, it seemed very evident to Joseph that the young pathologist was very much in love with his daughter.

'Not attending the hospital dance tonight, Rogers?' questioned the old man, who was, Brett noticed, wearing tails. Despite immaculate tailoring, he still looked like a gnome.

'Dancing is not much in my line, sir.'

Joseph Powell accepted his glass, saying: 'Linda will be disappointed.'

Brett smiled wryly. He thought it most unlikely that Linda would care and his expression said as much.

'Why not come along and join us, Rogers? It won't take you long to change and I'm

198

perfectly contented, meanwhile, with your fire and your beer.'

But Brett shook his head.

'You were Andrew McNeil's predecessor, weren't you, sir?' he asked suddenly.

'I was. And, talking of McNeil, I suppose you've heard the news?'

'What news?'

'About his marriage.'

A terrible apprehension clutched Brett's heart.

'McNeil's marriage?' he repeated with an effort.

'This afternoon. I was there—so, of course, was Linda! That is really why I came tonight. She is too afraid to face you, Rogers.'

Brett sat very still. From a distance he heard his own voice saying: 'She needn't be—I understand.' But it was not his own voice. It was the voice of doom, echoing from afar.

'I thought you would,' said Joseph Powell, watching the younger man carefully. He sipped his drink, then added casually: 'I said it was about time those two woke up, didn't I?'

Brett stared—dully at first, then with dawning comprehension.

'Which two?' he whispered.

'Why, McNeil and Hilda Gamlin, of course. Who else? Naturally, it was a quiet wedding. Very sudden, too. Apparently McNeil was passing the residents' wing the other day and saw some white heather growing in a window-box. It belonged to Matron—though what the devil heather and a window-box have to do with it beats me! But there it is—for some reason it opened his eyes. Linda told me the story, rather incoherently, in the midst of all the excitement down at the registry office—'

'Matron!' Brett gasped. 'And I thought—I actually thought—'

He covered his face, briefly, with his hands. Relief submerged him in an engulfing tide.

'For a young man of intelligence, Rogers, you are surprisingly stupid. You have a profound knowledge of things medical, and absolutely none of things emotional. You analyze and dissect and get the wrong answers. The more you understand microbes, the less you understand human beings.'

Brett laughed, a trifle shamefaced.

'She's a bit worried,' the gnome continued. 'Linda, I mean. Told me that McNeil's summons took her so much by surprise that she just shot out of the laboratory. They wanted us as witnesses, and from the way McNeil called us both it was in the nature of a Royal Command!' He took a crooked pipe out of his pocket and began to light it. As he puffed, he said in jerks: 'Better come along— Rogers—' Tossing the match into the fire he drew on his pipe contentedly and finished: 'To the hospital dance, I mean. It might make that girl of mine happier to know you forgive her. For some reason or other it means a lot to

Linda. Of course an old man like myself wouldn't be knowing why . . .'

And the gnome's bright eyes twinkled above his pipe.

But Brett had gone. He was in his bedroom, scattering clothes in all directions, hunting for dress studs and a clean white tie.

'Mind if I open another bottle?' called Joseph. 'I need fortifying for all the duty dances I have to cope with this evening. And by the way,' he finished as Brett shot from his bedroom to the bathroom, 'take a tip from me and don't dance with my sister Ethel. She'll march you round the room as if you were an army of Territorials . . . Where's the bottle opener?' he called.

'On the tray,' Brett shouted back.

The old man found it and continued conversationally: 'Although, of course, if you're marrying into the family you might as well get acquainted with the lot of us . . .'

Brett's tousled head appeared suddenly through the bathroom door.

'Me?' he gasped ungrammatically. 'Marry *Linda*? Do you really think she would?'

He sounded as if heaven had opened and tossed a golden trumpet down to him.

The gnome chuckled.

'Why not ask her yourself, Doctor, and find out?'

CHAPTER TWENTY-FIVE

The ballroom of the Town Hall was packed to overflowing. Brett experienced a moment of panic as he surveyed the moving mass of people, the colorful whirl of the women's dresses splashed against the magpie effect of dinner jacket or tails. There was a goodly smattering of navy and gold, too, and the fortunate nurses who had escaped night duty on this great occasion were having a wonderful time.

But how, in Heaven's name, was he to find Linda in all this crush? He saw Janet Humphrey floating by in a mist of blue, with Doctor O'Hara's black sleeve around her waist and her hand upon his shoulder. As she passed, there was a flash of red upon her finger—like a warm, pulsing flame. Even in his state of breathless anticipation Brett was aware that a transformation had taken place in Janet Humphrey.

'This way,' said Joseph Powell, and propelled Brett from behind. There was a dais at the far end, banked with flowers, and on it were a group of people, their glasses raised. Sir Christopher Herrick and other members of the hospital committee; dear little Lady Herrick, her arm through that of the shy little student nurse from Cunningham; Linda's stout, gushing mother—bejewelled and befurred; Doctor Chambers, smiling for once. During his halting progress round the ballroom Brett could not distinguish every member of the group, but as he approached he saw Andrew McNeil in the midst of it and, beside him, Matron. They were standing close together, smiling their acknowledgement of the toast being drunk in their honor. Brett smiled, too. They looked supremely happy—and supremely well matched. He wondered why he had never noticed that before . . .

And then Linda was beside him, and her father's quaint little figure bobbed across to his wife. Elizabeth's voice floated toward them.

'So *there* you are, Joseph! Where have you been? We are drinking a toast to Hilda and Andrew—get yourself a glass, dear, at once!'

If she was disappointed because her own daughter had not married the senior visiting surgeon, she had recovered very quickly, but perhaps (and Joseph was the only person who guessed this) it was because her husband had been telling her recently of the wonderful future predicted for the chief pathologist . . .

'Weddings are in the air,' said Linda softly. 'First the McNeils, and next the O'Haras. Haven't you heard about that? Mr. Bailey has been rather nasty about it, I understand, and tried to prevent Shaun from getting the weekend leave he applied for—but he got it, just the same. So I'm to act as witness again a week from now . . .'

'Stop talking,' commanded Brett, 'and come outside—'

'And then there's Meg—' Linda ran on. 'You know about her, surely? Andrew helped me over that. He gave that cocktail party so that she could meet Simon Wardour—we planned it over lunch that day, the two of us. The day you were so angry because I was late getting back—' Linda gave a tremulous little laugh and, greatly daring, added: 'D'you know, Brett, I almost wondered if you were jealous . . .'

'I was. Hellishly.'

A lovely color flooded her cheeks.

'Father told me what you thought—about Andrew and me. Oh, I didn't pump him! He volunteered the information after the wedding today.' Her voice shook. 'If I had known you believed that absurd rumor, Brett—'

'What would you have done?'

'I would have told you the truth.'

He seized her hands.

'Come and tell me—outside.'

She followed him meekly, her hand in his. Caught up in the swaying mass of dancers, he was forced to put his arm about her, and thus he found himself dancing, for the first time in years. It was surprisingly easy, with Linda, but this did not make him lose sight of his target. As they approached the exit they bumped into the immaculate figure of Augustus Bailey, dancing with Miss Corn. He bowed stiffly and continued on his respectable way. Linda suppressed a giggle and felt Brett's arm tighten about her waist.

'You have an enchanting laugh,' he whispered, and swept her through the main doors and out to his waiting car.

He drove down to the harbor. They travelled in silence, not glancing at one another, both aware that they stood together upon the brink of heaven and content to remain there. At length Brett stopped, and it seemed to Linda that in this breathless moment eternity and earth were one and they were alone together in the heart of it.

She turned, and saw Brett's eyes alight with question and hope. There was no need, then, for the words which trembled upon her lips, for the assurance and explanations which would come in good time. She was in his arms, and there she was content to remain.

*   *   *

From above, upon its proud hill, the Royal Rockport Hospital looked down upon them, but, as usual, it was interested in little but its own affairs—which was only natural, for it was a world in itself. There it stood, magnificently detached from the gay celebration at which three quarters of its staff were enjoying themselves; proudly aloof from their hopes and disappointments, their joys and fears. It had other things to think of, for although one half of the hospital slept, the other was very actively awake.

Down in Cunningham Ward Richard Herrick slept—dreaming, perhaps of Meg. In a few days he would be discharged and she would embark upon her great adventure with Simon Wardour, and after it was over the real Meg would come back to him . . . but he knew that however lovely the real Meg was, she could not be more dear to him than the existing one.

In the ward kitchen the night nurses brewed tea and did their knitting and talked enviously of the hospital dance and their more fortunate colleagues who were enjoying it.

'Lucky for Humphrey that the night sister got over her 'flu just in time,' said one.

'Did you see her before she left? My dear, I didn't *dream* she could look so lovely!'

'Someone told me it wasn't Mr. Bailey's car which came to fetch her, but a taxi. And who d'you think was in it? Doctor O'Hara!'

'No!'

' 'S'true! She's all washed up with dear Augustus—didn't you know?'

'I have it on good authority,' said a rather prim nurse, 'that Mr. Bailey asked to be released from the engagement.'

Hoots of derision greeted this statement.

'Judging by the way Doctor O'Hara looked at her as he helped her into the taxi, girls, *I'd* say it was the other way round!'

'Pour me another cup of tea, someone . . .'

A patient's bell cut into the companionable silence. With a sigh, a nurse rose to answer it. 'Why can't they sleep?' she muttered, and went on her way, while behind her another girl stifled a yawn.

'I sometimes wonder,' she said wearily, 'why I went in for nursing. It's so dull . . .'

We hope you have enjoyed this Large Print book. Other Chivers Press or Thorndike Press Large Print books are available at your library or directly from the publishers.

For more information about current and forthcoming titles, please call or write, without obligation, to:

Chivers Large Print
published by BBC Audiobooks Ltd
St James House, The Square
Lower Bristol Road
Bath BA2 3BH
UK
email: bbcaudiobooks@bbc.co.uk
www.bbcaudiobooks.co.uk

OR

Thorndike Press
295 Kennedy Memorial Drive
Waterville
Maine 04901
USA
www.gale.com/thorndike
www.gale.com/wheeler

All our Large Print titles are designed for easy reading, and all our books are made to last.